CRISIS ON CONSHELF TEN

MONICA HUGHES

When 15 year old Kepler Masterman, the first person to be actually born on the Moon, arrives on Earth for a six months visit he is greeted with some unexpected and unwelcome surprises. First of all, he can hardly breathe; and, at six times his moon-weight, he can barely stagger through the heavy earth atmosphere. 'This low-grav syndrome can be a problem,' someone says sympathetically.

But for Kepler the only solution seems to be another atmospheric change, and he joins relatives who live in an experimental underwater community – Conshelf Ten. In this extended frontier Kepler is to find all the excitement – and more – that he had originally hoped for on the earth's surface. His new-found cousin Jon, with his beautiful girlfriend, Hilary, are friendly at first. But why do they deny the existence of the strange swimmers who float through the ocean depths with no breathing apparatus of any kind? Who are the mysterious Gillmen, and what is the sinister plot that drives Kepler deeper and deeper into danger?

As he finally becomes aware of what is happening in Conshelf Ten, Kepler realises that the future of the entire world is threatened.

CRISIS ON CONSHELF TEN

MONICA HUGHES

REED BOOKS CANADA

First published in Great Britain 1975
by Hamish Hamilton Children's Books Ltd
Magnet paperback edition published 1981
Reprinted 1983, 1984 (twice), 1985, and 1986
Reissued 1989 by Mammoth
Reprinted 1991 by Mammoth
an imprint of Reed Children's Books:London

Published 1994 by Reed Books Canada:Toronto

Canadian Cataloguing in Publication Data

Hughes, Monica, 1925–
    Crisis on conshelf ten

ISBN 0-433-39214-2

I. Title.

PS8565.U34C7 1994   jC813′ .54   C94-932177-X
PZ7.H84Cr 1994

Printed and bound in Canada by
Metrolitho Inc.

To Jacques Cousteau
and His Fellow-Explorers
of the Silent World

AUTHOR'S NOTE

All the "facts" in this story, set early in the 21st Century, are either in the experimental stage, on the drawing board, or at least seriously discussed as possibilities today.

Though the world will undoubtedly have "gone metric" long before that time I have used the English system of feet and miles throughout, as giving a clearer picture to those of us unaccustomed to thinking in metres and kilometres.

CHAPTER ONE

I sat in the darkened view room of the space station and looked out at Earth. It was strangely familiar to me. The photograph of the blue globe with its whip-cream swirls of cloud hung in the Control Centre of Lunar Lab 21. There was a small copy of the same famous picture in our own living unit. To my mother and father it had meant home.

What was this Earth to me? It was a shining silver disc, waxing from crescent to full, and waning back again to crescent, that traversed the skies of our long lunar nights. It was the song my mother sang to me, the first child born on Moon:

> "Earth-shine, Earth-bright,
> Grant the wish I wish tonight."

But that was long, long ago. Mother had been dead for five years, and I, Kepler Masterman, son of Moon Governor, was actually going to Earth myself. Already I was over the first hurdle, the wearisome three day journey on the old beat-up Moon ferry to the space station.

It was great to stretch my legs again and enjoy the low-grav of the station's slow spin after the weight of the moon-rocket's acceleration. I looked down at Earth, so close I felt I could reach out and touch. What was down there? ... The

Sphinx ... the Taj Mahal ... Skyscrapers. All the fantastic things I'd read about. I looked at my watch. Fifteen minutes to wait.

Restlessly I left the viewing room and glided down the long passageway to the hub of the space station. In the VIP lounge I could see Father, surrounded by reporters. Time for one last goodbye to Moon.

Down the passage to the right here. The view room was empty, and I slid into a couch in the centre front row. The room was dark and the window was set in an angle that fooled the eye. It was as if nothing separated me from the black infinity of space and from Moon. It was so small now, my Moon, no bigger than the silver identidisc on the chain around my neck.

My eyes picked out the familiar features. The terminator, that razor-edge between night and day, arced down through the Ocean of Storms. The oblique sunlight etched clearly in black shadow the huge circle of Copernicus, and, to its left, right on the edge of the terminator, I could see Kepler, the crater in which Lunar Lab was built. Home! Down there a new Moon-day was just starting. The viewing ports of the Labs and of the living units would automatically darken as the brilliant rays of the sun stabbed down white-hard against the rocks of the crater. The heat-exchange units would slowly adjust from two weeks of warming up the buildings to cooling them, as for the next fifteen days the sun would shine down on Lunar Lab 21.

Down there at home the kids would be getting ready for the party. There'd always been a party at sunrise, ever since I could remember, and I was the oldest kid on Moon. The adults used to tease us sometimes ... "Imagine having a party every *day*!" But, heck, it was only twelve or thirteen times a year, and there was something special about the sunlight creeping so slowly across the surface of Moon, striking the peaks of the Apennines, sending shadows chasing across the Sinus Aestium,

10

each Earth-day a little closer, until finally the two long weeks of night were over, and we were bathed in sunlight again. The astronomers hated daytime, except for the solar experts. They couldn't see the stars and had to stay in their rooms catching up on their paperwork. But everyone else loved it, especially the kids.

I sighed and thought of Ann. Wonder who'd be taking her to the party? We'd stood at the air-lock to say goodbye. Ann had been crying and her eyes were red. But she was as beautiful as ever. There had been an awful lump in my throat as I blurted out the words.

"I'll be seeing you, Ann."

"Oh, Kepler, take care of yourself."

"Sure. You too, Ann. I'll write, I promise."

It was a terrible farewell. I'd worked out ahead of time exactly what I was going to say. It was terrific. It'd have bowled her over. But standing there by the air-lock I'd forgotten it all.

I squirmed at the memory and hoped that Ann wouldn't remember and laugh. Well, at least I could write. I knew I couldn't expect letters from Ann. Letter rates to Earth were crippling—so was the cost of everything that had to make the 240,000 mile haul. But I could write to Ann. That was one advantage of having the Lunar Governor as Father. I could slip my letters into the diplomatic bag and they would go rocketing to Moon with no questions asked. But six months away from home ... gosh, I was going to miss her. *That* was the disadvantage of having a Governor for Father.

The door swung open behind me, letting in a shaft of light and a babble of excited voices. There was a waft of exotic perfume. Real French perfume! The ferry from Earth must have arrived. These would be passengers on Moon Safari. This was a trip only for the very, very wealthy. In fact the tourist complex on the Sea of Serenity helped pay for some of the research expenses that Moon administration was unable to wring from the reluctant cashbox of Earth.

I slipped out of the suddenly crowded room and down the passage to the central concourse. Father was standing there. There were last minute goodbyes.

"Good luck, George."

"We're counting on you, Governor!"

"See you in six months, at the latest."

I walked beside him, trying to copy his casual stroll. I wasn't about to look like some country Rube even if it was my first Earth trip. But my first sight of the Earth-ferry threw me and my jaw dropped. It was magnificent, three times as big as our beat-up old Moon-ferries with their huge cargo holds and dingy cramped passenger quarters. Yet we had had to endure the lunar trip for three long days, and this was only going to take about three hours.

"Is everything on Earth this fancy?" I whispered to Father, as I snuggled down into the deep plush of my contour seat, and buckled my harness round me.

"Pretty much so—in the parts of the world you'll be seeing, anyway. It's a far cry from home, isn't it?"

Was it ever! I tried to imagine our living unit with a deep blue pile carpet and walls of cream stippled with gold, instead of the standard issue green vinyl floor and plastic-coated steel walls. When I was a kid I was always roaming into the wrong unit. They were all identical, and there just wasn't the money to ferry up from Earth the sort of things that would have made them look homey.

Soft music came over the intercom, and a stewardess in a micro-mini of some shimmering synthetic stooped over to check the fastenings of our safety straps. She had long hair that swirled around her face in the low-grav. It was of some strange shimmery colour that I'd never seen before. Her eyelashes were longer than seemed humanly possible.

She moved down the aisle and Father grinned across at me. "Close your mouth, son. You're going to have to get used to sights like that, or everyone will know you're just a moon-boy!"

"Wow, Father! Was she for real?"

"That's a good question, but one I've no intention of going into right now!"

His words were muffled by a metallic clanging. The ferry shivered delicately and then moved slowly out of its holding dock. I could feel my body pressing gently against the padded couch as the ferry surrendered itself to Earth-grav. It was amazingly quiet and comfortable. I'd hardly slept on the trip down from Moon, and now, in spite of myself, I found my eyes shutting.

It seemed only a few minutes before Father's voice woke me. "You're a pretty blasé traveller, Kepler! But you mustn't miss this sight. We're just turning into Earth orbit. Look!"

I craned my neck eagerly and looked through the port. I recognized the narrow spindle of central America, and then the steely shimmer of the Atlantic lay beneath us. It went on and on.

"The planet's all water!" I gasped.

"Seven-tenths of it is," Father agreed.

"But ... but. Oh, wow!" It was feeble, but what words could I have for it? A world that was seven-tenths *water!* Why, on Moon, water was harder to get than oxygen, much harder. Breathing was free. You could breathe as deeply and as often as you wished. Now that the hydroponic gardens were going we didn't have to pay for our oxygen any more. But water was something else. Every ounce of it was worth its weight in Moon minerals. Dirt was removed by electrostatic filters in the labs and living units. Washing was a luxury and drinking a special delight.

There was no free water on the Moon. Every ounce we used was extracted in the refinement of the ores we sent down to Earth. And the mining companies charged us for it—every drop! I had grown up thinking water was the most precious stuff in the Universe. Now with my own eyes I could see that Earth was covered with the stuff—slopping over with it.

We orbited across North Africa and Arabia. From my port I could see the island-spangled blueness of the Indian Ocean. Then the Pacific. I felt suddenly tired and a little sick. What sort of a place was this Earth and what were its people like? Half a world made of water, and yet they had charged us for every single cup. I shut my eyes and turned away from the port.

"You feeling groggy?" Father's voice was sympathetic. "They're starting their braking orbit, and I guess you'll really notice the weight difference. Don't worry. It'll get worse before it gets better. But it will get better. Just hang on!"

To the Earth passengers from the space station I suppose the discomforts were minimal. Their apparent weight increased to double and momentarily three times their normal weight. I had not realised until this moment what my birthright of one-sixth Earth weight was going to mean when I tried to return "home". It was like a barrier separating me from all these other people. Already I weighed six times my normal weight. As the braking continued it increased to twelve times, to ... The weight on my chest ... I couldn't breathe. I felt as if my brain was going to burst.

When I came back to my senses the enormous pressure had lifted. I felt heavy and very tired. I lifted my head and looked blurrily around. We had landed! There was a bustle of unstrapping harnesses, collecting belongings. I struggled with my own safety straps, and Father leaned over to help me. The expression on his face told me I didn't look good.

"Lie still, Kepler You've had a nose-bleed. I'll get a stewardess to help."

"I'm okay, Father." My tongue felt thick and the words were blurry. The stewardess hurried over. Her strange metallic hair no longer swirled around her face, but hung heavily over her snoulders. When she bent down to wash my face a

lock swung forward against my cheek. It had a strange tanta-
lizing perfume.

"I can do it," I muttered thickly, trying to take the cloth
away from her.

"You just lie still, sonny. I'm just going to get you an icepack. You really took the 'Gs' badly. You'll have two beautiful
shiners in the morning."

Sonny! How old did she think I was, anyway? Two black
eyes ... oh, brother! That was really starting out on the right
foot. Look out, Earth. Here comes Kepler Masterman—on a
banana skin!

She glided back with the icepack. How could she move so
lightly on this heavy planet, I wondered. She looked no heavier
than a grain of moondust.

She spoke to my father. "Governor, the Press and TV are
waiting for you. Are you ready to leave the ferry yet?"

"Oh, sure. I'll come right away." He swung himself up
from his couch and stretched. He was a big man, my father,
and muscular. I wondered if I'd ever catch up. I was at the
weedy stage, and in spite of secret body-building in my own
room I wasn't making much headway.

"Strange feeling going up to 170 pounds again. Don't think
I like it much. Kepler, lie still and take your time. I'm sure
this young lady will look after you."

I watched his broad back down the aisle and through the
hatch, and then I took off the icepack and swung my legs
down to the floor. My head throbbed a bit, but it wasn't too
bad. Standing was tougher, and walking was a nightmare of
wading through glue. I gritted my teeth and practised, one
foot and then the other, up and down the aisle, holding on
to the seat backs for support.

Six months on this planet. How was I ever going to make
out? I saw the stewardess watching me from the galley door.
I wished she'd go away, but when she saw I'd seen her she
came down the aisle towards me.

"I could get you a wheelchair," she volunteered. "This low-grav syndrome can be a problem. It's happened before, you know, though I guess you're the first person who's never experienced Earth-weight in his life."

"I'm going to be fine, thanks. It just takes a little practice, that's all."

"Of course. Perhaps you'd like to tidy up before you leave?"

I took her hint and plodded back down the aisle to the washroom. Good grief, I was a disaster area! I took off my jacket—how crudely cut it looked in comparison with the Earth fashions I'd seen on the ferry, and what rough material. Then I washed the rest of the blood off my face and combed my hair, what there was of it. It looked like a convict cut by Earth standards, but it would grow. There were red smudges under my eyes, but the shiners the stewardess had promised hadn't shown up yet.

I put on my jacket and plodded down to the exit hatch. I hesitated, my hand on the ramp rail, looking at the crowd of exotically dressed reporters, cameramen and casual bystanders milling around my father. It really was a new world down there at the end of the ramp.

"Good luck," the stewardess said softly. She wasn't a bad sort, really, only a bit old to understand. I managed a smile, swallowed and walked down the ramp to join my father. I was drowned in a storm of voices. How loudly these Earth people talked, as if they were constantly trying to shout each other down.

"Governor, would you say the differences between Earth and Moon people are irreconcilable?"

"I certainly would not. On the contrary I am convinced that with a clearer understanding of our problem, the differences between us will be settled amicably."

"What do you intend to do if the U.N. vote goes against you?"

"I am not even considering that possibility at the moment."

"Governor, how long do you intend to spend on Earth this trip?"

"I anticipate that it may take as long as six months to settle our differences, though of course we could strike lucky."

"Why could your representations not have been made from the Moon?"

"They frequently have been! With singularly little result. It is only too easy to forget or shelve the pleas that come from 240,000 miles away, when there is plenty of pressing business for the U.N. closer to hand."

"Governor, are you alluding to the threatened rebellion of the under-water cities? Will you comment on the position of the Conshelfers as compared to your own?"

"I was speaking in generalities. As a visitor to Earth it would be extremely impertinent of me to comment on a domestic situation about which I know little or nothing."

"One last question, Governor. Now you are back on Earth again will you tell our listeners—which is really home to you, Earth or Moon?"

"That's a difficult question to answer. All my cultural ties are with Earth. But, like the immigrants who flocked to the New World and shaped it into a nation, I guess I must say that it is in this Newer World, Moon, that my present and future lie. My son was born there. My wife was buried there. My work is there. Yes, gentlemen, it is good to be back on Earth. But Moon is home!"

He saw me standing jammed among the reporters and casually gave me his arm. We walked together across the sun-splashed concrete of the landing pad. The sun was gently warm on my body and our shadows ran out ahead of us, soft, muzzy-edged. I looked up. The sky was a delicate blue with fluffy cumulus clouds, just like the ones in my old video tapes. They sailed gracefully across the sky, unbelievably beautiful. A sudden white shape plunged and screeched. I jumped and clutched Father's arm.

"What was that? ... A bird?"

"Yes, Kepler. A sea-gull."

I walked along, breathing real air, not the canned stuff. It was strange being out of doors without a space-suit, scary but exciting. It looked as if Earth was going to be fun. If only my legs didn't ache so ...

"Is it far to the magnetrain, Father?"

"Hang on, son. It's right ahead."

Once aboard with my feet up I didn't feel so much of a country cousin. The magnetrain had been developed on Moon, where the absence of any atmosphere had precluded the use of conventional jet, hovercraft or internal combustion engines. Up there we had perfected the magnetic lift system of propulsion and our trains networked the lunar surface with silent pollution-free speeds of 500 miles an hour.

The idea had been enthusiastically adopted by an ecology-conscious Earth, and one of the items on my father's agenda was to negotiate an acknowledgement in terms of royalties of the Lunar discovery.

I lay back and thought of the pyramids and the Taj Mahal, the temples of Angkor Wat and the mysterious jungle buildings of the Incas. Would six months be time enough to see it all?

CHAPTER TWO

Two weeks later I was still lying on my back, this time in the hotel swimming pool, watching the light filter down through the sky dome and send reflected patterns dancing over the walls. There was soft music. There was *always* soft music. From that first moment of boarding the Earth ferry soft music had followed us everywhere. I was getting pretty tired of it.

I practised my flutter kick. It was getting quite good and my leg muscles were definitely developing. So they should after fourteen days spent exclusively in the pool.

It had been the hotel doctor's idea. We met him on our arrival at the U.N. Hilton. He took charge when my knees gave way and I collapsed in the middle of the crowded lobby. Me, the clown, with my black eyes and spaghetti legs.

"Spend all the time you can in the pool. You've got to develop those muscles and get your system adapted. Can't swim? No ... I suppose there's not much opportunity on the Moon. Never thought of that. Well, you'll learn. We'll give you a hypno-sleep course to get you started and give you confidence, and we've an excellent instructor in the hotel."

So here I am, I thought, spending my precious six months on Earth getting acquainted with one green and blue tiled swimming pool about thirty by a hundred feet. I had looked forward to writing to Ann about the Sphinx and Angkor Wat, but what was I to write about now? I cupped my hand through the water and I felt the pressure and splatter of drops against my skin. Water! That was wonderful anyway, almost worth the price of Earth gravity!

The pool was always deserted at this cocktail hour. It was the time I liked the best. I felt more comfortable alone. The bruises under my eyes had faded and my hair was no longer so unfashionably short. I'd bought a couple of the light silky play outfits that all the kids seemed to be wearing. But I still didn't fit in.

Oh, it was my fault. I guess that when you got down to it I had come to Earth expecting to be accepted as the Moon Governor's son and the first-born from Moon and all that stuff. It made a hit with the little old ladies, all right, but I could feel I wasn't cutting any ice with my own age group, so I sort of crept into my shell and lurked there. When the pool was empty I could be myself and horse around, and maybe even sing. So I was kind of annoyed when the swing door pushed open and this girl came in.

She was different from anyone I'd yet seen on Earth. I trod water and frankly stared. She had long red hair with gold tints in it, exotic, but you could tell it was real, not like the ferry stewardess'. Her skin was pearly clear and pale. That was different too. All the people around the hotel were either tanned brown or a strange brick red colour. I thought it looked hideous, but I guess it was fashionable, for they lay for hours in the sun, rubbing stuff into their skins and getting redder and redder.

But this girl was as pale as a moonbeam. She stood at the far end of the pool, slipped shoes like fins on to her feet and put a sort of strange mask over her eyes and nose. She slid into the water without a splash, and I could see the fluorescent orange of her swimsuit flash like a goldfish to and fro under the water.

I watched her for perhaps ten minutes. Then she surfaced close to me, pushed the face-mask up on to her forehead and smiled. Her eyes were a very dark blue and slanted up slightly at the corners. There was a dimple by her mouth.

"What's the matter? You look as if you'd seen a ghost."

I tried to pull myself together. "How ... how do you do that?"

"Snorkel? Nothing to it. Want to try?"

"Could I?"

"Why not?" The goldfish girl swam to the side and with a push of her arms was out of the water and sitting on the edge in a shimmer of water-drops.

"Come on out. I'll show you how a snorkel works."

"I'll swim over to the steps."

"Oh, come on." She put out a hand and pulled me out of the water. "What's the matter? You sick or something? You can't skin-dive unless you're in really good shape, you know."

"It's not that." I felt the hot colour mounting in my face. "It's just that I'm from Moon. I'm low-grav."

"I see. Well, you'll adjust in a couple of days, I expect. Then you could try skin-diving."

"I don't know. I've been here two weeks already, and it doesn't seem any better."

"You're kidding! How long have you been up on the Moon?"

"Fifteen years."

"Fifteen? But ... I mean, how old are you?"

"Fifteen."

"Well, a genuine moon-baby. There's a thing!"

"Don't call me that .   please."

"What do you call yourselves, then?"

"Sellenites, mostly."

"*Sellenites* ... that doesn't sound like anything. I know. I'll call you lunatic! See you around, lunatic." She pushed her face-mask on, slid under the water and was gone before I could think of a really insulting answer.

I sat on the edge of the pool, glowering at the golden shape in the water. Lunatic, indeed. She made me burn. I heard the water splash as she climbed out, and the bang of the swinging door, but I didn't look up. I didn't look up when the door swung again. Let her come to me and apologize. I felt a hand on my shoulder. It was Father. I scrambled up, confused.

"I'm sorry. I didn't hear you. Aren't you dining at the U.N. tonight?"

"I am, but I may be late and I wanted to talk to you, Kepler. Let's go and sit down."

He walked over to the group of deck chairs arranged under some potted palms. I plodded after him and sat down, massaging the soles of my feet. Much more of this heavy planet and my arches would be as flat as pancakes.

"You can't go on struggling with this gravity, Kepler. I'm sorry it's turned out this way. If only your mother were still alive you could have stayed on Moon with her."

"It's okay, Father, it couldn't be helped. I know I'm not old enough to be on Moon-staff, and Earth would never authorize me to stay up there as a non-productive unit. I had to come with you. But they'll never let me go back without you for the same reason. Gravity or no gravity. I'll just have to bear it."

"I had another idea. Remember your Aunt Janet ... my photographer sister? She and your uncle Ted work in one of the undersea labs, Conshelf Ten. They have a son, Jon, about your age. How would you like to spend the rest of your Earth time living under the sea with them? They'd love to have you."

"I wouldn't have this weight problem?"

"No. The Conshelfers spend much of their time outside. You'd be weightless there, and of course the amount of swimming you'd do would be terrific for your muscles and circulation. What do you think?"

"It'd be better than this. I wonder what Jon's like?"

"I haven't seen him since I was on Earth last, years ago.

But they're really looking forward to meeting you. You'd have lots of company. It could be quite an interesting experience."

"It sounds good, Father. But what about learning all that underwater stuff?"

"SCUBA. I've had a talk with Ted on the marine phone. He thinks it'll be easy for you. You're used to a contained environment and controlled breathing from Moon walks, so you won't be subject to panic or claustrophobia. Your cousin Jon has a friend just finishing University up here. He'll be returning to Conshelf Ten in about a week, and he can escort you down, besides giving you SCUBA lessons before you go."

"Sounds terrific, Father. I'd like to go. What's the guy's name? Where can we find him?"

"Hilary Delaney. He's staying here. I'll leave a message at the desk for him to get in touch with you. Now I must go. Kepler, I *am* sorry about the pyramids and the Taj Mahal and all those other things."

"Maybe I'd have been disappointed. They're only buildings. And living under the sea sounds really keen. The kids back home will never believe it. Not just bathing in water—living in it!"

On my breakfast tray next morning was a note: "Meet you in the pool six pm. HD". It had obviously been scribbled in a hurry on hotel stationery, and I could get no clue as to HD's personality from the scrawl. It would be great to meet someone my own age. The U.N. Hilton must be the most splendid building on Earth, next to the Taj Mahal, of course, but it seemed to be mostly occupied by worried delegates and wealthy widows of uncertain age. The young people I'd seen around made me feel so stupid I'd about given up on human companionship.

Which made me think of Moon. I'd better write to Ann while I had the chance. At last I had something exciting to write about. That took care of most of the morning, and after lunch I lay on the water-bed in my suite and tried to sleep. In spite of the air-conditioning it felt muggy and close as if all the richness and extravagance was using up the air. I dozed a little on and off and looked at my watch impatiently.

Finally it was five-thirty and I climbed into my trunks and robe and went down to the pool. It was empty as usual. Time to practise my flutter kick before Hilary came. I tried swimming under water, but everything was blurry and I couldn't keep my sense of direction. How on earth did the sea-dwellers manage? I surfaced with a splutter as I ran out of air, and grabbed at the edge of the pool.

"Not bad for a lunatic. Did you get to swim on the Moon, or was it only dust-baths up there?" The cool voice was full of laughter. It was that bratty girl again. She was kneeling on the edge of the pool, her copper-red hair falling forward over her face as she looked down at me. I looked blankly back, unable to think of a single smart thing to say. I turned away, ready to swim across the pool, but she put out her hand and grabbed my arm.

"What the ...!"

"Come on. Don't play games. We haven't got all day, and you've an awful lot to learn."

My mouth fell open, and as I sagged in surprise she shifted her grip to my hand and pulled me out of the water. That girl had muscles! I sat there dripping, gaping at her.

"Well, you *are* Kepler Masterman, aren't you? You got my note? I'm Jon's friend—Hilary Delaney. What *is* the matter?"

"I ... we thought you were a boy," I stammered.

"Good grief. Do I look like a boy?"

"No, of course not. I mean ..." I tried to pull the shreds of my dignity around me. "We misunderstood. Hilary *can* be a boy's name, you know. Do you really live under the sea?"

"Sure do. Nearly all my life. I'm just topside for a course in land biology. We've got very good marine schools, you

24

know, but some things you just have to study in their natural environment. Otherwise killer whales couldn't have dragged me up here. It's such a rat-race here, and so dusty and noisy and hot. Down there it's all so different. Well, we'd better get started, lunatic!"

"Okay, water-baby!"

"Oho!" She turned from the pile of equipment beside her and grinned at me. She was an awfully bossy girl, but I couldn't help noticing how nice her teeth were and that she had a little dimple at the left corner of her mouth. "Pax, okay? I won't call you lunatic again if you don't call me water-baby."

"Okay, Hilary."

"Now listen hard, Kep. There's an awful lot to learn, and you mustn't practise except when I'm here and I'll be busy with exams all this week so we'll have to make every moment count. You must never make a mistake. No second chances under the sea. So listen.

"Now this is your face-mask. You always wet it before putting it on and then it won't steam up. Without it you can't see. We have to have a layer of air in front of our lenses in order to focus. The lower part of the mask covers your nose. Okay? Now these tanks hold compressed air."

"They weigh a ton!"

"Don't worry. Under water they're nothing. In fact you have to wear a weighted belt in order to keep under even with tanks on. Down at Conshelf depths we breathe different mixtures of gases depending on where we're working. But up here compressed air is all right. Now this is the mouthpiece. Put it in, against your teeth, that's right. When you suck in you get air at the right pressure for the depth you're at. That's because of this demand valve here. Always check it's working properly. It's the most important piece of your equipment. If you start running out of air it gets harder to draw in. Then you turn on this emergency valve. That's the next most vital thing in your equipment. Now let's put the stuff on and try you out."

We worked down in the pool every evening of the next four days. I learned how to take off all my gear on the bottom of the pool, and how to get it back on again under water, clearing the mask and mouthpiece of water by blowing into them. I learned how to buddy-breathe, swimming from one end of the pool to the other, sharing Hilary's mouthpiece and air, and then we did it again with Hilary sharing mine. She taught me how to look after my own equipment.

"Everybody has his own, with a special place to keep it. It's life and death, you see."

I nodded and Hilary looked at me curiously. "You're not even faintly nervous, are you, Kep?"

"No. Why should I be? I took my first Moon walk with Father when I was seven, and I learned pretty young about life-support systems. On Moon we had less edge than you have undersea. You can't hold your breath, or buddy-breathe while you head for home. A leak in your suit that you can't repair in thirty seconds and you're through."

"Did accidents happen often?"

"Not really. Maybe half a dozen times. But you don't forget. The industrial accidents were the worst. There was one when I was ten or eleven. A mine shaft blew. The experts had calculated that the walls were plenty thick enough, but it turned out to be a particularly fragile rock that the geologists had missed. The whole shaft went out like a balloon in about fifteen seconds. Yeah, Earth people don't really understand what it's like living in near-vacuum."

"Kep, I owe you an apology. I've been unbearably bossy. I don't know how you've had the patience to put up with me."

"No other options?" I suggested and grinned at her.

"Ouch! The thing is I don't like Topsiders. They come sightseeing on the Conshelves. They litter the place up with garbage and get themselves into stupid predicaments that we have to risk our necks getting them out of. Then they go home and vote on the next undersea appropriations without any real idea of what it's actually like living and working under three or four atmospheric pressures."

"You sound as if there were drawbacks to living down there."

"Oh, don't get me wrong, Kep. I wouldn't live anywhere else in the world. The peace, the freedom, the beauty. But ... oh, I guess it'd be like an Easterner back in the nineteenth century telling a western frontiersman how lucky he was to be out in all that fresh air with no responsibilities!"

"You don't have to sell me. It sounds as if our positions were amazingly alike."

We got on much better after that, and it seemed almost no time till the afternoon when Hilary met me by the pool, her arms full of books.

"That's it, glory be. Exams over. For better or worse I'm through. If you'd get dressed now, Kep, we'll have time to get your equipment from the Marine outfitter. Then we'll get an early start in the morning. I can't wait to get back home!"

I went up to change. My street clothes were laughably different from Earth fashions, but it hadn't seemed worth buying anything more than play clothes when I spent all my days in the pool. Luckily Hilary didn't seem to notice. We took the automatic motorway to the docks. From the dizzy height of the tenth-floor track I could look down at the shoppers scurrying like ants far below, and up at the pinnacles of skyscrapers glowing in the sunset. It reminded me of dawnlight on the Apennines, and I felt suddenly alone and very far from home.

"Could I take you out to dinner tonight, Hilary?"

"Why, yes, I'd like that."

"You pick the place, will you? Somewhere high up, perhaps, where we can see the Moon."

She looked across the car at me and smiled gently. "I know just the place."

The car swung off the main track in response to its programmed card, and stopped at a bay extending out from one of the skyscrapers. Hilary stepped out unconcernedly, but as I followed I looked down through the metal grille-work and saw the street swaying dizzily below. I shut my eyes and swallowed. When I opened them Hilary was holding open the elevator door. We dropped in a few breathtaking seconds to street level, and she whisked me around the corner to the Marine Outfitter.

It was a fascinating place, crammed with ropes and lamps, spears and airtanks. Hilary firmly took charge, and in a very short time I was fitted out with wetsuit, belt, flippers, depth gauge, compass, tanks harness, mouthpiece and face-mask. I blinked at the price, but Hilary seemed unconcerned, and I meekly pulled out Father's credidisc.

The man bowed. "That will be fine, sir. We'll have it all delivered to the hotel first thing in the morning."

"I know the cost is terrible." Hilary took my arm as we left the store. "It's one of the things Topsiders don't take into account when they compute Conshelf salaries. But you'll be glad of that suit. Conshelf Ten is in fairly cool water, and that model wetsuit has an automatic chemical heating unit. You'll be as warm as toast no matter how long you stay out. I remember in the old days we used to have to thaw out under a hot shower after only a couple of hours in the water."

Back at the hotel she spoke to the man at the main desk, and then turned to me with a smile. "He's arranging a table at the Eastern Beacon. I'll go and change. I don't suppose you have evening things, do you?" It was the first time she'd mentioned my Moon fashions. "You can rent something easily. Just ring for the valet. I'll see you in an hour, okay?"

I felt awkward explaining what I wanted to the severe-faced man who answered my bell, but he seemed unconcerned.

Perhaps Earth people often travelled around the world without special clothes. But when he returned and laid the things out on my bed I had a dreadful feeling that it was a conspiracy to make fun of me.

"You're ... you're sure that's right?"

"Quite definitely, sir. This year's mode for youth's evening apparel."

I swallowed, looked at my watch and hurried into the clothes, dark blue tights and a silky tunic with silver embroidery. There was a cloak too, of darker blue lined with silver. I looked at the stranger in the mirror. Well, it wasn't too bad, really, with my pale skin and dark hair and eyes. Just weird. At least I was thin—it would have been dreadful on anyone fat. I looked at my watch again. Time to go. Credidisc. Room key. I took a deep breath and headed for the elevator. Nobody sniggered. In fact nobody seemed to notice me at all.

Hilary was just coming down the passage as I entered the tenth floor lobby. I stood and frankly gaped. I'd never in all my fifteen years seen anything like her. She was wearing a dress of pale gold that fitted, well, like her swim suit. It had long sleeves and a kind of wide high neck, and just above the knees the material seemed to break into thousands of shimmery threads that swirled to the ground in a cloud of gold. She had knotted her hair at the back of her head somehow, and she suddenly looked years older than me. But as I walked slowly forward she grinned at me, the same old grin, and I relaxed.

It was after eight o'clock before we were settled on the observation floor of the Eastern Beacon. Through the transparent walls and roof we could see the stars burning above us, and their reflection in the city lights below. I ordered with Hilary's help, and sat back to enjoy my last Topside evening on Earth.

"Look, Kep." Hilary suddenly leaned across the table. "See why I picked this restaurant." I followed her eyes and saw

29

Moon rising in the East. It seemed to appear all at once out of the ocean, a gibbous waning Moon that scattered silvery scraps of itself in a jigsaw pattern across the sea.

"Try these binoculars, Kep. Courtesy of the management."

I blinked my eyes clear and looked for details of home. The terminator arced down through the Seas of Serenity and Tranquillity. The rays of Copernicus splayed out across the surface, and caught in their web I could just see the lesser crater of Kepler. Lunar Lab 21, unit A. Home. I looked for a long time.

Finally I put down the glasses. "Thanks, Hilary."

She squeezed my hand. "You're welcome, Kep."

The music soared around us.

"I ... I'm sorry I can't dance in this grav."

"That's fine. I don't much enjoy dancing on land myself."

"You dance down *there*?"

"Ha! Wait and see. There's a whole new world waiting down there for you, Kep, much more beautiful than this one. Look over there. Where the lights of that liner show. See? Past there just a little way, twenty miles off shore and ten fathoms under ... that's *home*!"

CHAPTER THREE

I took a last quick look around the hotel room. Most of my stuff was stored in Father's suite. What I needed was in a small watertight bag that Hilary had brought me, just toiletries, warm underwear, sweater and slacks, a photograph of Mother and Father and a snapshot of Ann.

"Anything else Jon can lend you—you're much the same size," Hilary had said.

"Are you engaged to Jon, or ... anything?" I blurted it out abruptly, but I had to know.

"Or anything?" Her light voice was mocking. "How old-fashioned you are, Kep. We're only fifteen."

"On Moon we're promised at thirteen. I guess there are so few of us the psychologists were afraid of feuds and jealousies wrecking the programme."

"Not to worry about wrecking people's personal lives, of course. Then you're—how did you put it—promised?"

"Yes. Ann is the daughter of the chief comptroller. She is fourteen. She came to Moon three years ago."

"When will you be married?"

"Eighteen is usual—when I go on staff."

"Oh, wow! Well, it's your life. Come on. Let's get going." She whirled out of the room in a swirl of red-gold hair, and I realized she'd never answered my question about her and Jon.

My goodbyes to Father were hasty. There was a vital committee meeting on mineral resources in half an hour. I looked at his strong face with the wise grey eyes and the translucent pallor of moon-dwellers, and impulsively hugged him. We hadn't been apart since Mother had died.

"Perhaps you can come up and spend a night here once in a while."

"I don't think I can, Father. Hilary explained it to me. Conshelf Ten is under three times atmospheric pressure, and the gases we breathe are forced into the blood under that pressure. So long as you stay down you're fine, but if you want to surface you have to do it very slowly to allow the gases time to expand slowly and escape through the lungs. It takes over twenty-four hours in a decompression chamber."

"I didn't realize. What would happen if you surfaced straight away?"

"Then the gases would expand and froth out as bubbles in your blood. Hilary said it would be like opening a bottle of pop on a hot day—but that didn't mean anything to me. Do you get it?"

"Yes. That I can remember. Kep, take care. It sounds as if pressure can be as deadly as vacuum."

"Don't worry, Father. I'll watch it."

"Then it's goodbye for some months, anyway. I'll try and speed things up at this end."

"We can talk by phone, any time you're free, Father. Good luck with the conference."

Hilary appeared at the door. "Come on, Kep. I've an automatic waiting to take us to the harbour."

I looked over my shoulder as we went towards the landing bay. Father was walking towards the elevators, surrounded by secretaries and advisors. He looked very much alone.

Out past the harbour, the sun danced on the waves. I could feel it stinging my skin and making tears come to my eyes.

"Won't be long," Hilary shouted. "These hoverjets are fast."

It was a small plastic launch with four seats. As it skimmed without a tremor over the choppy sea I looked in disbelief at the speedometer. 100 ... 150 ... 180.

"I don't believe it. I thought air and water had such terrific drag."

"They do. I suppose compared with moon-coasting this is nothing. But this design makes the air and water work for us instead of against. There are wedge-shaped planes under the hull with channels that force the air under the craft to lift it above the water, and at high speed the air is forced into the jet to give the thrust. They're noisy but neat. Look, we're nearly there." She touched the driver's arm, and pointed.

Dead ahead of us was a buoy, a plastic-covered cage with radar reflectant panels. The engine died and the hoverjet sank slowly down to the surface, and rocked to a stop close to the buoy. We had already got into our wetsuits at the dock, and had only to put on weight belt and flippers, fasten our belongings to our waists and swing the SCUBA harness into place. Hilary checked my apparatus and turned for me to check hers. I slipped on my face-mask. Hilary spoke close to my ear.

"Remember—it's no different in principle from the pool. Stay close and do what I say. Air okay?" I sucked my mouth-piece and nodded.

"Then down we go."

She flipped backwards off the craft and rolled under the surface. I took a deep breath, looked around at the bright sea and the sun dancing on the water, at the grinning sunburnt face of the hoverjet driver, and then followed her.

There was an instant of shock as the waves buffeted me unexpectedly. Then my week's training took over and I slowly kicked myself down. Hilary was waiting for me, her hair billowing like the stewardess's in low-grav. She waved her hands slowly and pointed down. I nodded and followed her lead. How quiet and still it was. I found myself moving languorously through the water. I glanced at my depth gauge.

Thirty feet ... I felt suspended in a cool blue-green weightless world.

Hilary looked over her shoulder at me. I wanted to grin, or laugh, but my mouthpiece was in the way, and I had to content myself with the traditional thumbs-up gesture of all's well. She finned down into the darkness and I followed her.

Here was the bottom at last. It wasn't really so dark once one's eyes grew accustomed. It was a gentle twilight world, and there, shining like a comet-tail, was a line of light along the sea bottom. Hilary followed it, and presently I saw another light-line coming in to meet ours. Then another. Ahead was the shadowy loom of domed buildings. I realized that the markings were like airfield lights, and they all radiated out from the centre of Conshelf Ten.

There were buildings all around us now, and people crowding close, patting Hilary on the arm, waving. Too much to take in. It was all I could do to concentrate on breathing regularly, and keeping Hilary in sight. She turned and beckoned me. A couple of strong kicks under the shadow of one of the domes, and she vanished in a flurry of silver bubbles. Cautiously I followed and looked up. There was a circle of light above me, like a mirror. It looked hard and impenetrable. I kicked and let my body rise.

Sound and light poured over me like a shower. I felt hands pulling me out of the water. I spat out my mouthpiece and pulled off my face-mask. I had arrived! I was sitting on the floor of an almost spherical room, my feet dangling through a hole into the water. I looked down in amazement.

"The water doesn't come in. There's no airlock, but it doesn't come in."

Hilary laughed and swung her feet in the water. "Oh, it's not like the Moon, where you're all the time trying to stop your atmosphere from escaping into vacuum. The weight of the water at this depth is three times atmospheric pressure, so we maintain dome pressure at the same three atmospheres.

The forces balance. The air doesn't go out and the water doesn't come in. Now, I'm off. Skin out of your wet-suit and take a shower, Kep. Jon will be along to help you stow your stuff."

"Where are you going?"

"Home. To my mother and step-father. Tell Jon I'll be over for dinner." She raised a hand in goodbye, and slid down into the water.

I stood up and looked around me. The dome, which I supposed was made of metal, was lined with a warm orange plastic, and divided by six-foot high partitions. In front of me was a bulkhead, blank except for a cabinet with the ominous label "first-aid and resuscitation". I wriggled out of my SCUBA gear, and wetsuit, and explored through an opening in the partition to my left. Yeah, here was the shower. I relaxed under the warmth, only to be startled by a sudden icecold needle spray. I dodged out into the next cubicle, looking for a towel. There were none to be seen, but a warm current of air played on me from all sides. In a few minutes I was dry and feeling great. I still clutched my bag of clothes. Should I put them on here? Poking my head through into the next area I saw against the curved dome wall a padded bench with a light-bracket above it. As I hesitated a cheerful voice shouted from somewhere outside the dome.

"That you, Kepler?" A tousled head poked around the curved doorway leading into the next room. "Oh, good. I see you found your way around. I'm Jon King. Welcome to Con-shelf Ten."

"Thank you." I found myself speaking formally. It was strange to find myself with relatives, where before I had known nobody except the inhabitants of Lunar Lab 21. I stared at my new cousin.

"We're alike, Jon. Almost like brothers. It's strange."

"Once your hair grows. Does everyone on the Moon shave his head?"

"Not *shave*," I protested. "Just short. It's really much more efficient."

"Oh." Jon looked blank. I wondered why. Then he smiled. "Get your clothes on, Jon, and we'll go meet the family."

"I haven't used this thing," I gestured at the lamp on the wall.

"That's all right. You don't need it now. Once a day is enough. It's ultra-violet in the wave-lengths that keep your skin germ-free and provide vitamin D. In the early days the Conshelfers found that when their skins were wet so much of the time cuts and scratches wouldn't heal properly and they were susceptible to fungus infections. These lamps make all the difference. Just remember to wear those goggles and to set the timer."

"I'll remember. How long have you lived down here, Jon?"

"Eight years. That's when Conshelf Ten started. Mom and Dad worked in some of the older undersea labs, but I stayed Topside with my grandmother."

"Which life did you like best?"

"Wow! Need you ask! Come on, and meet the family."

I had skinned into sweater, slacks and moccasins while we talked, and now I followed Jon through the low curved doorway joining the two hemispheres.

"It's an automatic watertight door—just in case anything should go wrong with the pressure system. Not that it ever has," Jon explained.

"Like the ones on Moon." I tried to keep my voice casual. Those tons and tons of water above my head made me feel kind of spooky. I looked around. On my right was a neat little kitchen, and to the left a dining area, while ahead, taking up the far half of the dome, and partly hidden by the head-high kitchen partition was the living room.

It was painted a warm attractive creamy colour, and the lighting was hidden by storage units along the curved walls. It was certainly different from the military sparseness of Moon dwellings. The curved wall-seat was covered in red, and the hooked rug was patterned in flames of gold, orange and dark red.

I realized I was gaping like a lunatic and went forward, blushing, to shake hands with my aunt and uncle. But there was no formality with Uncle Ted and Aunt Janet. She flung her arms around me and hugged me.

"Oh, Kepler. It's so good to see you at last. Let me look at you. You're so like George. Isn't he, Ted? Jon? Oh, how silly—you've never seen your Uncle George, have you, Jon? But you've seen him on TV. Isn't Kepler like him?" She pulled me down to the wall-seat and sat beside me. "Now tell me what you think of Conshelf Ten?"

"Oh, Mother!"

"It's kind of early to tell, Aunt Janet. But this room is beautiful—that rug!"

I'd said the right thing. She beamed. "I hooked it myself. Took two years. But it was worth it to cheer the place up. These living units—seen one, you've seen them all. But you'll know all about *that* from Moon-living."

"This is luxury compared with home. We don't have curtains or carpets or soft chairs. And everything is painted the same depressing sort of dark green."

"Why must government units always have such hideous colours? I'm sure beautiful paints are as cheap as ugly ones. We had to fight for these colours, and all our other amenities, I can tell you. You should fight for your rights up there on the Moon, Kepler."

"Mother, that's what Uncle George is down here for," Jon put in patiently. "Though I guess it's about more important things than the colour of the paint in the living units."

"Quite right, Jon. We'll never be able to afford luxury bulky items. That's understandable, with the freight charges on 240,000 miles. But we do want the right to make our own decisions about how we live and work—choose our own paint

37

colour, for instance." I smiled across at Aunt Janet, who beamed back.

"There, you see, Jon. Kepler and I understand each other very well. The colour of the paint *is* important. It's a matter of principle. Now, how about some coffee and sandwiches." She darted out of the living room.

Jon smiled. "Don't mind Mom. She sounds kind of irrelevant sometimes, but she's a really great marine photographer."

"I believe it. She's Father's sister, after all!"

"I heard that. Good for you, Kepler. Jon, why don't you show Kepler his room while I heat the coffee."

Jon uncurled himself from the rug and led the way through another doorway into a third dome. This looked more like our moon units since it was divided into separate rooms.

"Bathroom on your left. Parents' room ahead. Your room on the right here, mine next door." Jon rapidly opened doors. "Up that ladder into the ceiling to the main storage unit and the escape hatch."

"Escape hatch?"

"Each dome has its own. It's a two-hatched lock. In case of sudden pressure drop or rupture of the dome you scramble in and shut the hatch behind you. Then open the other and swim to the nearest unit."

"Have you ever had to use them?"

"Only for practice. But they're there—like fire extinguishers. Don't worry, Kep. These domes are really solid. Fibreglass-covered aluminium. The pressure system has a back-up system and an alarm. Believe me, Mom would never have hooked that rug if there was the remotest chance of it getting wet!"

I licked my dry lips and managed a laugh. After all it was no worse than space, and I'd been accustomed to that since birth. I looked round my room. It was small compared with my hotel suite, but palatial compared with my bedroom in Lunar Lab 21. It was a wedge-shaped room, with a bed along the straight left wall, and a desk and bookshelves in the wall containing the door. The curved wall was fitted with a padded wall-seat and storage units. The light was soft and indirect, and could be dimmed or turned off from the door or the bed. If I could ever get used to the feeling of pressure this was a nice place to have.

Lunch was really different. It was tastier than the freeze-dried and synthetic moon-food, but lighter and less cloying than the elaborate stuff I'd been eating at the U.N. Hilton.

I reached for another cookie and Aunt Janet beamed. "That's what I call an appetite. What is it? Oh, fresh tuna salad and sea-weed cakes. The baking is made with fish protein concentrate instead of flour. You can't raise it, but at this pressure I couldn't make light cakes anyway. We settle for things like tortillas and cookies."

"Do you have to eat all seafood? Do the Topsiders make you?"

"Oh, no. But Topside food is terribly expensive because of all the shortages, and it's not so nourishing. When this Lab was started we decided to try and become as independent as possible. I think we're all hooked."

"Specially with a cook like Mum," Jon interrupted. "Now let's suit up and I'll show you over Conshelf Ten."

That night I lay on my bunk in the small bedroom. It was completely silent. The air-conditioner was inaudible, and only the tell-tale streamers fluttering from the ceiling grille told me it was functioning. There was no screech of magnecar, no whine of elevators, no sirens in the streets. I lay under sixty feet of water in a cocoon of quiet. What was that Victorian song? ... Rocked in the Cradle of the Deep. But down here was neither calm nor storm. It was a world without weather, like Moon.

I felt restless and breathless, as if the weight of water were pushing the walls of the little room in on top of me. I slipped out of bed and opened the door. A shaft of light from the living room patterned the floor of the passage. I could hear low voices. It was Jon and Hilary. I had left them in peace, pleading a most untrue sleepiness, when Uncle Ted and Aunt Janet had left to visit neighbours. It seemed airier with the door open. I padded back to my bed and lay there, playing back the day's events in an effort to get sleepy....

The layout of Conshelf Ten. Let me see ... In the centre the Undersea Lab, consisting of four cylindrical arms, spread out from a central dome, like a deficient octopus. Central had a store and a cafeteria, a big communications centre, conference and class rooms and a library.

Cylinder One contained the food-lab, where the most efficient methods of growing, harvesting and processing seaweeds were tried out. The scientists there were responsible for raising fish in corrals like cattle, and processing the protein for a hungry world. What had Jon said? "The continental shelves almost equal in area the whole of Africa, and just one acre of properly prepared ground can produce a harvest of fifteen thousand pounds of shellfish protein. You can raise four thousand tons of seaweed per square mile." No need for famine now!

Cylinder Two was the bio-chemical Lab. Here the chemicals derived from shell-fish, sponges and other ocean animals, and plants were tested for their potential as pain-killers, antibiotics, cancer-fighters, heart stimulants. It sounded exciting, but scary, since many of the sea-animals had poison more venomous than the deadliest snakes on Earth.

Cylinder Three was the big money-maker, and into its projects the Topside Government poured its allotments of funds. Here research was carried out into the economical mining of the sea, and the extraction of oil and precious metals. Listening to the lab technicians talk I was reminded of Moon, where we had to scrounge for every cent of experimental money for laser research, electronics, plasma, while Earth poured funds into mineral exploration, and clamoured for more and more raw materials.

Cylinder Four was the Lab where Uncle Ted worked as a Marine Biologist. It was the most fascinating to me, but the shabbiest and with the least funds.

"But they can't requisition our brains," Uncle Ted had laughed, as he'd shown us round. Here they studied the ecosystem of water, fish and algae, noting seasonal temperature changes, quality of the bottom, the potential feeding ground to the number of each species.

Conshelf Ten, Uncle Ted told me, was situated on an old coral reef, far offshore and removed from any major river outlet. Some of the other Conshelf Labs spent their days clamouring for pollution abatement, but to little avail. Air pollution had been legislated against years before and the internal combustion engine altered out of all recognition. Politicians breathed the air. They could tell the difference. But the rivers, moving with cleansing swiftness out to sea, the sea with its apparently infinite capacity for absorbing punishment—and garbage. That was something else.

"I'd like to take the whole pack of politicians and sit them under the outfalls of some of our rivers," Uncle Ted had exclaimed in disgust. "Maybe they'd appreciate what Topsiders are doing to our sea!"

Dolphin and porpoise intelligence and communication was one area of this lab that was adequately funded, solely because of its possible military use. "Though the day they succeed in perverting a dolphin's mind to help the men on one side and consider the 'others' to be enemies—that's the day I resign from the human race," one of Uncle Ted's colleagues had exclaimed.

I sighed and moved around in bed. It seemed so quiet and far removed from strife, and yet down here on the bottom of the sea it seemed that the human problems were the same ones, the moral decisions as difficult....

41

Back to the layout of Conshelf Ten. Radiating out from the lab complex were the homing markers we'd followed on our way in. They were of magnetic tape, treated with bio-luminous paint, so that besides responding to any homing device they shone with a green glow as any pressure wave excited them. They extended like the strands of a web for a mile in each direction, and to the inhabitants of Conshelf Ten they must have been like the street signs of a city.

Clustered around the lab complex in two concentric circles were the living units, A to H forming the inner circle, and J to T the outer. Each unit was totally independent in air and fresh-water processing, waste disposal and communications, and each had its own nuclear energy uni-pack.

"This way we have as many life-support systems as we have living units. It's frightfully expensive, and the first conshelves were all linked to central support systems, in spite of pro-tests from the personnel. Then about sixteen years ago there was a severe earthquake that jolted one of our sites in the Gulf of Mexico. Fifteen scientists died and the twenty-three who escaped suffered permanent injuries from the sudden pressure change when they had to escape to the surface on a tankful of air. After that disaster we got our way."

"You sound bitter, Jon. But you weren't even born then, were you?"

"No, but Hilary's father was there, and he was killed, and one of her older brothers."

As I remembered that conversation I thought of Hilary, so beautiful and yet with this bitter wayward streak in her that made me feel uncomfortable and inexperienced. As I thought of her I realized that the voices in the living room were louder, that I was hearing a conversation that had turned into a quarrel.

"Hilary, I tell you violence isn't the answer."

"Jon, you're as weak as the elders. Why won't you see? It's the *only* answer. We have all the cards. If we only play them right and show no signs of weakness we'll get our demands."

"People are going to get hurt."

"People always get hurt in revolutions. It's the price we have to pay."

"Hilary, you can't mean it!"

"I'm sorry, Jon. I can't play games about something so important. It's the way I feel and you've got to know it. Nothing must get in the way—nothing!"

"Hilary, I can't bear to think of you mixed up in that violence." I could hear the misery in Jon's voice.

"Will you join us, Jon? Will you?"

"I can't, Hilary. Not yet anyway. I must have more time to think. But I won't give you away, I promise."

"You'd better not, Jon. Not a word. Not a gesture. Because if you did, they'd kill you, and there'd be nothing I could do to stop them."

I slipped quietly out of bed and softly shut the door. The voices and the light were blotted out. I went back to bed and eventually to sleep.

CHAPTER FOUR

I woke suddenly with a feeling of pressure and suffocation. In my dream I had been back home in Lunar Lab 21. Was it a pressure leak, or a blow-out? I sat up fast and swung my legs off the bed, listening for the alarm signal. There was no sound in the darkness around me. My six-times Moon-weight dragged at my legs. I woke up properly and remembered where I was.... Then it hit me.

The vacuum of space held no terrors for me. I had been raised with air-locks and space-suits, and the danger of blow-out. But this ... this ton-weight of water over my head. Sixty feet of water, every thirty feet equivalent to the total weight of the atmosphere at the surface, every square inch of it pressing against my body, diminishing me, crushing me.

I gasped and pressed my hands together. They felt chilled and slippery. The sweat ran coldly down my face and neck. It was hard to breathe, terribly hard ... It was getting harder with every breath.

With an enormous effort I got to my feet and stumbled through the lock into the living room. It was in darkness and I leant against the wall, gasping, trying to get my bearings. Through the uncurtained porthole window I could see in the greenish blue luminescence of the sea a flurry of little fish. The shadow of a big groper loomed against the glass and was gone. I licked my dry lips and tried to master my thoughts

... I've got to get out ... there's no way ... don't panic ... I've got to get out.

I stumbled through the next lock into the service dome, and knelt down by the hole in the floor. Ten inches below the floor surface the water mirrored the dome light, blankly silver. It was like a locked door.

I lay down on the ridged plastic floor with my face over the edge of the hole, and trailed my hand in the water. The surface broke into silver droplets and ran off my fingers. Water. The most precious stuff in the Universe. And I was caving in because I was living under it! I thought of the searing dryness of the great dust plain between Kepler and Copernicus. I thought of the hard cold emptiness of Space....

After a while my breathing steadied, and the shaking in my hands went away. I sat up and dangled my legs in the water. There was a splash and an echo of rings on the surface. I jumped. A soft nudge to my feet. And another. Half a dozen small fish crowded the entrance port checking up on my dangling legs. I laughed out loud, and felt I was part of the Universe again. I took some water in my hands and washed the dried sweat off my face. There was a noise behind me. It was Jon.

"You okay, Kep?"

"Sure. Did I wake you? I'm sorry."

"It's all right. I was sleeping with half an ear open, wondering if you'd get the first night heebie-jeebies. Most people do, even Conshelfers who've been away from home for long."

"Really?" It was good not to have to feel ashamed. "How does it ... I mean, what happens?"

"Well, some people try and break out through the dome walls or the ports. That's all right, because you can't. It'd take a bomb. But one or two head straight for the surface and that's really dangerous. We keep a close watch on newcomers till they're over the crisis. You see, you've already been down here over twelve hours. Your blood is saturated with gases

45

under three times atmospheric pressure. By the time you hit the surface the gases would have expanded so that your blood would be supersaturated and the bubbles would be coming out of your blood like soda pop. In your joints—it can cripple for life, or in your heart or lung tissue—and that can kill."

"Lucky I didn't," I grinned at Jon. "Though it did occur to me. Thanks for coming to look. I suppose we ought to go back to bed, though I must say I don't feel a bit sleepy."

"No need. It's around 4.30. That's a good time for seeing the whole bio-system in action. Later in the day the fish go deeper and the night-feeders sleep. Come on. Let's suit up."

We ducked out, and I followed Jon away from the domes. As soon as we had left the dark loom of the buildings and were among the old coral and rocks of the reef Jon switched on a light, and the blue-green world changed at the touch of a switch to a world of fantastic colour and movement.

The night-feeding starfish moved slowly away from the light like leggy ballerinas. An octopus ducked shyly down behind a rock, his hunting blue turning to a dirty brown blush. A spiny lobster raised his claws to the light in warning, and then crawled away, his golden brown shell reminding me of the pictures of mediaeval armour in my history microfilm back home.

The Conshelf habitat, Jon had told me, was on the site of a coral reef that had been alive many centuries ago when the sea floor was near enough to the surface and the water warm enough to sustain the delicate coral polyps. Now sunk sixty feet below the surface the old limestone homes of the coral had become the shelter for wrasse, damselfish, jacks and a myriad of smaller creatures.

As we watched they responded to Jon's flashlight and slowly came awake for another day. The small fish flickered out and formed a tight shoal, responsive to the least pressure in the water, darting from side to side in a single movement when threatened by a movement of our hands, or flipping into the protective folds of coral if we approached too close.

The larger fish seemed to move independently of each other, but each kept to a certain section of water and rock, as if the area had been surveyed and mapped. We couldn't read their invisible boundary signs, but to each fish it was obviously clear, and his neighbour was always there to enforce the territory.

Now and then a bigger fish would loom like a storm cloud over the active bottom. A flurry, and all would be still, with not a fish to be seen. How they ever caught enough to feed their great bulks was a mystery to me.

I drifted a few inches above the bottom, glorying in my weightlessness. It was better than free fall, for there was none of the sensation of helplessness against recoil, nor the inability to move about freely. I was as in control of my environment as an eagle soaring cliff high.

Jon turned off the light. For a moment darkness crowded in and I put out my hands to steady myself against a rock. Then my eyes adjusted and slowly I became aware that the quality of the light was changing, that far overhead, in that other world, the sun was rising on a new day.

The separateness of that other world no longer bothered me. I was no longer alone. I felt alert and secure. Jon had given me a re-breather, which absorbed the carbon dioxide out of our exhaled air, and sent the air back to be re-used with a carefully monitored addition of oxygen. With this system only the smallest tell-tale bubble escaped, and freed from the constant noise of one's own escaping bubbles I could listen to the language of the sea, a faint barrage of sound, clicks, whistles and groans, the early morning chatter from the awakening fish colony.

It seemed only a few moments before Jon tapped me on the shoulder, pointed at his watch and made the motions of eating. We had been out for over three hours! As we swam back towards the loom of the buildings I noticed that each of the units had its distinguishing letter painted on the side and again by the entrance port; so I wouldn't be embarrassed by diving into the wrong house.

Here was G, and like an old hand I jack-knifed under, and broke the surface of the water. I scrambled up the ladder and sat on the edge to struggle out of my re-breather unit. I still had that weight problem, but I managed to get it off without help.

"Thanks, Jon," was all I could say, as I rinsed off my mask and mouthpiece.

Jon looked across at me and laughed. "I can tell you're sold. No more heebie-jeebies?"

"Not a one. Jon, you won't say anything to Aunt Janet and Uncle Ted?"

"Of course not." Jon looked blank. "You didn't have to ask." That was the second time I'd gone wrong with Jon. I was a long way from understanding these Conshelfers, I realized, and filed it for reference.

Breakfast was delicious—fried cakes, like pancakes, though Aunt Janet said they were made of fish-meal concentrate with an ingredient derived from kelp to replace the eggs, and with a delicately flavoured syrup poured over them, developed from some other kind of seaweed. Hungry after my three hour swim I ate and ate.

"We're going out for the whole day, Mother," Jon remarked as he mopped the syrup off his plate. "Could you give us a packed lunch? Hilary and I want to show Kepler the corrals and kelp beds."

"That's an awful lot for one day, Jon. Are you sure Kepler's up to it?"

"I feel great, Aunt Janet," I interrupted hastily. "Being weightless out there makes all the difference. For me just sitting around is more tiring, honestly."

"We won't overdo it, Mum. We'll take a sled and extra

tanks. We'll have enough air for eight hours. We can take it slowly and still be home for supper."

"All right, dear. Be sure to leave your travel plan with Control. I'll make your lunch now and you can take Kepler through the long-distance check list."

"Check list?"

"You'll see." Jon grinned. "Suit-up in five minutes. First I suggest you make use of the wash-room facilities. It'll be three hours before our first way-station stop."

When I went into the service module I found that Jon had a mound of equipment spread out on the floor. There seemed to be an awful lot of it, far more than Hilary had ordered for me at the marine outfitters topside. Jon held a plasticised card in his hand.

"Okay. You suit up first. I hope you've got a heated suit? Good. Trust Hilary to get the best! Now on your left wrist, watch and depth gauge. Right wrist, compass and sonar alarm...."

"Sonar?"

"It picks you up on the radar screen back at Control—when you're in the water, not in the domes. If you get into trouble, press this knob and your friendly neighbourhood porpoise will home in on you and get you out of trouble."

"You're kidding, of course ... Aren't you?"

"Absolutely not. It's an acoustic device that our trained porpoises recognize. Of course it's no good if you've run out of air. Even a porpoise can't help you then, not at this depth. But they're great if you lose your sense of direction. Just like great big St. Bernards."

"St. Bernards?"

"A dog. It's not important. Sometimes I forget how much you don't know, Kep!"

"I'm pretty hot on Moon lore, Jon. I wonder how you'd rate up there! What's next, anyway?"

"The mike. Round your neck, against your throat—that's it.

49

The receiver is in your hood. Slip it on and see if you can hear me. Okay? This way we can talk to each other comfortably under water. They don't have much range, but it beats hand signals or trying to talk under water. You can do it— sound carries well under water, but the bubbles get in the way, and you have to get rid of your mouthpiece, of course. Now your weight belt. Food kit on the left side, specimen bag on the other. Knife around your right thigh, just above the knee."

"What's it for?"

"Maybe we'll get some shellfish for dinner! Actually it's a safety measure. You never know when you might have to cut your way out of a problem. Though it's better not to get into trouble in the first place. Anyway we always carry them. Now your breathing gear, same type as we used this morning. Always keep a lookout for the tiny bubbles escaping from this valve. It lets you know that the fresh oxygen is coming through to mix with your rebreathed air. And *this* indicator darkens if your carbon dioxide level is getting too high. Keep an eye on it."

"We didn't go through all this this morning?"

"No need. We were never more than a lungful of air away from a dome. Today we'll really be on our own. Now check me with the list as I tog up. I'll take a flashlight on my belt, but otherwise it'll be the same as yours."

I watched carefully as Jon suited up and then followed him through the exit port. We swam past the inner circle of living units, and Jon picked up a loose rock and tapped on the hull of a unit in the outer circle. Almost immediately a figure slid down through the exit and joined us. It was hard to recognize Hilary with her bright hair hidden in a black rubber hood.

"Hi, boys. You're in good time. Where first, Jon?"

"I thought we'd take Kepler up by the corrals and then over to the kelp beds. We can eat at Way-Station 24, and either come straight back or the longer way at the ninety foot level. Okay?"

"Sounds great. I picked up the sled and three extra breathing units from stores last night. It's parked below." She pointed down and in the flat blue-green light I could see the bright yellow paint of the sled. It was little more than a metal frame with several bulky packages strapped to it. Across the front was a steering bar, and on either side of the frame hung loops of nylon rope.

"I'll drive," said Jon and lay on his stomach on the sled, grasping the bar with both hands. He turned a switch on the central column. A faint hum came to my ears.

"Grab a hold, Kep."

As I reached for one of the nylon ropes the sled stirred, raised itself off the bottom in a flurry of silt, and skimmed along a foot or so above the bottom.

"It's a water-jet," Hilary's voice sounded unexpectedly in my ear. "The same principle that jellyfish and octopi and so on use. Instead of muscle power to push the water through we have underwater batteries. They're good for a full day's work before recharging."

We skimmed along through the water at about three miles an hour. My right hand firmly held the nylon rope, and the water tugged gently at my body as I drifted along beside the sled. On the other side Hilary was holding a similar loop. Between us, on the slender metal structure, Jon steered. It didn't feel insecure. It was wonderful, like childhood dreams of flying. I felt free and powerful.

I looked at my wrist compass. We were skimming northward, and Jon was holding the sled about four feet off the bottom. It was impossible to judge distances in this alien world, but we had been skimming along for twenty minutes, which I reckoned should be about a mile, when I noticed that we were following the line of a plastic pipe laid along the sea bottom.

51

"Oil?"

"No. Compressed air. See ahead and to your left. The corrals."

I had read dozens of westerns on microfilm, and I had a pretty clear picture from old Zane Greys of fenced grassland with cattle galloping around.

"Corral?" I blinked at the shimmering silver wall that blocked the way ahead. "What in the world?"

"Come on. We'll park the sled here and show you."

We drifted to a stop and sank to the bottom. I followed Hilary and Jon up to the base of the wall. The wide pipe we had been following ended in a valve and a T-joint, and I could see when I swam close that the small pipes running to left and right were evenly perforated along their upper edges. An unbroken thread of silver bubbles poured upwards towards the surface from each hole.

"It's a fish fence," Jon explained. "Same idea as a Texas Gate, which you can cross but the cattle can't. Fish have poor eyesight, but a fantastically developed sense of touch. They have a line of nerve endings along each side of their body, and this lateral line can detect minute pressure changes. To them the streams of bubbles appear to be a solid wall. They'd no more try to swim through than you would try to walk through the side of the dome."

"What would happen if one of them tried?"

Jon laughed. "I don't know, Kep. It's never happened."

"I can't see a single fish." I peered up. The silvery bubbles reflected the light like a mirror.

"We'll ask the herdsman if we may go in. Wait a minute. He should be somewhere about." Jon swam off and came back in a few minutes with a boy of about our age. Jon introduced us and we shook hands formally.

"It's okay to go in, so long as you don't linger over the barrier. I've got three millon prime herring in there, nearly ready for market. Through you go."

Jon and Hilary swam through the barrier, pulling me with them. There was a momentary tingling, and then we were inside, surrounded by the shadowed forms of masses of fish. Overhead the water darkened as a huge shoal of them skimmed by. We were completely ignored as the fish moved to and fro in their never-ceasing quest for food, brushing past our bodies. I was afraid to move in case I hurt one. Jon signalled and we turned and plunged through the barrier into the almost empty sea on the other side.

"It's almost unbelievable. How do that many fish get enough to eat?"

"We set up our corrals wherever the ocean currents bring in the richest supply of plankton. It doesn't take long to hook up the bubble pipes. They're plastic and move easily under water. The porpoises help us herd in the fish we want and cut out the predators. We have almost no losses and the yield is enormous."

"Are there many corrals on Conshelf Ten?"

"We usually have about a dozen, set up at different depths and temperatures, of course. Where the Gulf Stream curves in towards the shelf we can even raise tuna, but up in the northwest sector it's mostly herring and cod, which thrive in cooler waters. Let's go back to the sled if you've seen enough, and we'll show you the kelp forest."

We climbed aboard and Jon took us in a wide arc to the right. He kept the sled level at the seventy foot mark, and as we skimmed along I could see the shelf drop away beneath us into impenetrable darkness.

"We're near the Abyss." Jon's voice sounded hollow in my ear. "This canyon we're crossing cuts right in from the ocean depths. You must never come out here alone, Kep. It's too easy to forget and go too deep. And down there is for deep-divers and submarines only."

"What would happen to a person down there?"

"In the Abyss? Right now six hundred feet is our limit for

skin-diving with special training and apparatus. That's a pressure of nineteen atmospheres: nineteen times as much gas can be dissolved in the blood as at sea level, and the effect of each gas on the body is nineteen times as great as at sea-level. Up top you can tolerate three per cent carbon dioxide in your breathing mixture—down there one sixth of one per cent will knock you out. More than one or two parts of oxygen per hundred will cause convulsions and death. It's a very different world."

"Why do people try to go down? Is it worth it?"

"You bet. We need every square mile of ocean we can develop. Right now we can only utilize the shallow parts of the continental shelves, but we've got to expand beyond that. The mid-oceanic Ridge has an area equal to all the land-masses put together. But it's too deep for us now. But some day ... we have to consider adapting our own bodies, changing surgically, or possibly even by mutation...."

"Jon!" Hilary's voice was sharp. "Don't let your enthusiasm carry you away. We should be bearing west again. We're well past the corrals."

"Sorry." Jon sounded embarrassed, almost aghast. I suddenly remembered the argument I'd overheard the night before. What had Hilary said? ... "they'd kill you if anything leaked out and there'd be nothing I could do to stop it."

What was going on down on Conshelf Ten? What was Hilary involved in that was so dangerous and secret? It was obviously no good asking them—I'd have to do my own investigating if I wanted to find out anything more. But I was only a visitor and it was none of my business.

I looked ahead. The water was cold and clear, and Jon was easing the sled up a slope running towards the shore. My depth gauge indicated sixty feet, then fifty. We levelled off and turned north. Ahead of us a dark mass loomed up, absorbing what little light there was at this depth. It reminded me of pictures I'd seen of the giant forests of the old days.

As we approached I could see the individual stems of kelp, rising thick and smooth, olive brown. They moved to and fro as far overhead their fronds were tugged by wind and waves. I reached out and touched a slippery stem. As it stirred I felt connected in some strange way to that far off world of light and sun and wind fifty feet above our heads. I looked up. Against the light the kelp was a pale gold colour.

Jon's voice interrupted my thoughts. "We'll have lunch at the way-station and then explore. Okay?"

The sled veered west again and in a few minutes I could see on the sea-floor the familiar lines of bio-luminescent tape leading to a small plastic dome, anchored to the base-rock. It had the number 24 painted on the outside and I remembered the numbers on the big Conshelf map back on the Communications wall at Central.

We dived under the dome and up through the entrance port. It was good to wriggle out of the tightness of wetsuit and hood, and breathe straightforwardly again. I stretched and looked around me. A wide padded bench ran round half the dome, and the other half was screened off, one quarter being a washroom and shower, the other a small galley, with a cupboard labelled "emergency supplies". High on the wall was a telephone. Jon went straight across to it, lifted the receiver and announced our names ... "and we're going on to explore the kelp beds after a rest-stop."

We showered and dried and ate the lunch which Aunt Janet had prepared for us. It was a collection of savoury-tasting rolls of food wrapped in what looked like black plastic, but which the others assured me was edible seaweed. It had a tangy salty taste that went well with the blander fillings.

"The Japanese have eaten seaweed for centuries," Hilary explained. "We Conshelfers have borrowed some of our best recipes from them."

When the meal was over I lay back on the padded bench with a contented sigh.

"Tired?"

"No, not really. Tell me about the kelp. What are you cultivating it for? What actually is it?"

"It's a plant with a root system called a hold-fast and fronds like leaves. Some giant kelp have stems five hundred feet long. They have bladders filled with gas along the fronds to keep them near the top of the water—they need the light for photosynthesis, like most land plants. They're native to the Pacific Coast. We just have an experimental plot here, about three square miles, I suppose. Kelp's enormously valuable for trace-minerals, and for several basic medicines and foodstuffs, so we're hoping to turn it into a cash crop up here. If you're ready we can suit up and take a closer look."

As I wriggled back into my wetsuit Jon said, "Stick close to us when we get out in the kelp bed, Kep. It's very easy to get lost."

I felt myself flushing, but I said nothing and went on getting into my suit. It was a bit much the way these two treated me like an infant. Sure it was strange territory, but I'd been exploring the atmosphereless surface of Moon for more than seven years. I was no fool.

We slipped through the exit port. "Shall we take the refill breather packs?" Hilary asked as we passed the parked sled.

"Let's not bother. We've got over half an hour's air left in these," Jon answered. "Let's explore this bit and if we want to go farther we can pick up the packs later."

Gliding through the cool water I felt my anger melt away. A faint light filtered down from above, and the smooth stems of kelp slipped by. Jon turned his flashlight on a hold-fast and showed me the myriad tiny crabs, shrimp and fish that made their home in the root systems of the giant plants. I lay along the bottom, my face close to the hold-fast, watching the busy life of the inhabitants.

"Come on, Kep." Hilary's voice was impatient in my ear.

"There's no hurry. Let the guy look."

I ignored the voices and swam slowly along the bottom exploring one minute habitat after another. Hilary's voice came to me again—bother these ear-phones.

"Kep, take care. Don't swim where the stems are so close together."

I wished I could cut off the sound and be completely alone in this new world I was discovering. "Oh, hush," I said aloud.

At that moment a current of solid water picked me up and slammed me into the thickest part of the kelp forest. I found myself somersaulting over and over. I tried to get control, but there was no direction, no up or down. I was getting breathless. I nearly lost my mouthpiece. I let myself go limp and let the water take me where it willed. Finally the wild surging died down and I sank towards the bottom.

CHAPTER FIVE

I looked around, trying to get my bearings. The water was like soup, turbid with sand and mud. I forced myself to relax, waiting for the water to clear. After an eternity I could see my outstretched hand. I waited till the water had cleared for twenty feet. Then I looked round.

The smooth stems of kelp were close about me in every direction. There was no sign of Jon or Hilary. I called out to them, and then called again. I wanted to scream their names, but I knew that if they were anywhere in range the high frequency radio would pick up even a whisper.

I listened, straining my ears. The only sound was that of my own breathing. Where were Jon and Hilary? How could I find my way back to the way-station or Conshelf Ten without them? I called their names again and again. All was silent. Perhaps at long range my transmitter was directional. I began to turn slowly round, calling out ... Hilary ... Jon.

In response to my hand movements my body began to turn to the left, and then suddenly stopped and spun slowly back again. I struggled and tried to turn again, but it was as if I were imprisoned in elastic bands, which softly but definitely resisted every movement I tried to make. I looked down at myself. I was suspended about three feet off the bottom, with strong stems of kelp wrapped tightly around both my ankles and my left arm and shoulder. I pushed and tore at the tough slippery stuff and finally managed to wriggle out of the arm hold, but no matter how I fought I couldn't release my legs.

I found myself breathing hard ... panting ... and consciously slowed down. My Moon training took over. I knew there was death in panic. Breathe evenly. Conserve energy. Make a plan....

Something was nagging urgently at my memory. Something Jon had said. What was it? ... "We've got half an hour left. If we need more air we'll pick up the other packs later." How long since Jon had said that? How long had I been examining the life of the hold-fast? Ten minutes? Twenty?

I called again, and held my breath while I listened for a reply. What was the range of this thing anyway? How far had that wild current carried me from the others? I could be miles away in any direction.

Well, it was a nasty thought. But if I were really on my own I'd better smarten up and think while I still had time. Panic chased coldly through my body, and I hung on, shivering. Then as suddenly as it came it was gone and my mind was crystal clear and fast.

I reached for the knife, strapped to my right thigh, and slid it carefully out of its sheath. The kelp stalks were infuriatingly tough and slippery, and several times I came close to slicing into my leg. I sawed away. My eyes darkened. It was getting harder to breathe every moment. I sucked desperately at the mouthpiece, and remembered the emergency supply.

I turned the valve. The new oxygen was wonderful. My head cleared instantly. The knife had slipped from my hand to the sandy bottom. I reached down, hanging like an acrobat from the binding kelp stems. There it was. Reach out. One inch more. There....

I somersaulted round and sawed away. One stem gone. I kicked my right leg free. How long would the emergency supply last? Was it included in the half hour that had been in the tanks? Or was it a premium? Go on sawing. The knife was getting blunt. There. At last.

The stem snaked away from my left leg, and I turned cautiously round, careful not to catch the closely growing stems on my re-breather pack. Golden brown, smoothly gleaming, the kelp swayed around me, each stem a twin of the next. I remembered that there were three square miles of the stuff.

I had two choices, to stay where I was until I ran out of air, which wouldn't be long. Or I could swim in what I hoped would be the right direction until I ran out of air.

Either way it wasn't much of a choice. I looked at my compass and began to swim slowly south towards the habitat, trying to conserve my air and energy.

Down in this directionless world all my trust was in the tiny pointer on my wrist. I longed to be back on Moon with the Sun or stars to signpost me home. Instead I was in a world of eternal twilight with no features, no guidelines on the way.

I called again to Jon and Hilary. Was that an answer? I stopped swimming, held my breath. No. Just wishful thinking. Whatever had caused the wild current had scared the fish, too, and I had not even their clicks and whistles for company. There was nothing but my own heart beat, and the faint riffle of bubbles from the tell-tale of my re-breather.

I remembered the porpoises. Now they were my only hope. What had Jon called them? St. Bernards. That was it. I pressed the signal on my right wrist. I listened but it was on no audible frequency and I couldn't tell if it was working. I had to take that on trust too. I swam slowly south towards Conshelf Ten.

My arms and legs were as heavy as lead and I was getting sleepy again. I pulled the air into the depths of my lungs. Exhaled. Pulled it in again. No good. That was finally it. My oxygen was used up. What a stupid way to go, I thought slowly. What a stupid stupid waste....

Something butted into me, startling me awake. A porpoise at last. But it's too late now, my friend. No, not a porpoise. A MAN.

I was saved. We could buddy-breathe to the nearest way-station the way Hilary had taught me. I was okay. I reached out greedily for my rescuer's mouthpiece and found my wrists grasped and held in an iron grip. I was skimming through the water. Fast. Faster. But I had to have air. I croaked a plea for help and turned to reach the mouthpiece of my rescuer.

My head snapped back in shock, and for a moment my darkening eyes cleared. The man was covered from head to foot in a silvery close-fitting material, like the skin of a salmon. His long hair floated darkly behind him in the water. I saw his features clearly, the straight nose, the well-shaped mouth, the eyes slightly slanted.

I knew him. I recognized him. Yet I knew that in my wildest dreams I could never have seen him before. For this man had no breathing pack, no mouthpiece. Just before I blacked out I saw him draw the water into his mouth, and I saw the gills, silvery on either side of his neck, expand and flush pink as they took the life-giving oxygen out of the water.

Do I remember, or was it just a dream? There was warmth and lights, and hands pulling me out of the water. There was a stream of clean air pouring into my lungs. I remember the weight of the plastic cup over my nose and mouth. Remember that my eyes cleared and I could see the domed ceiling. I turned my head. I remember ... I *think* I remember the smoothly cut features of my rescuer, his hair darkly red under the dome light. For just as my eyes opened and my head turned towards the exit port he slid under the water and was silently gone.

I half raised myself from the padded bench, letting the face-piece of the resuscitator fall to the floor. The shimmer of water in the exit port was reflected off the ceiling of the dome, smooth and unbroken. I fell back on to the bench and slept.

When I next woke I was lying on my back looking up at

the softly lit curve of the roof. It was like a moon cave, only much warmer. I moved my head, and then sat up. I'd been stripped down to my trunks, and was on the curved seat against the dome wall, wrapped around with blankets. On the floor beside me was the resuscitator. I was alone in the dome. Where was my rescuer?

I got cautiously to my feet. For a moment I was giddy, but the feeling passed. How long had I been here? According to my watch almost two hours had gone by since I'd last looked at it, some time during my struggle in the kelp bed.

It was strange. I felt as if I'd been asleep for days, and yet I was still groggy. Hungry, too. Perhaps food would help. I walked cautiously to the galley. Gosh, my legs were weak. I riffled through the emergency supply cupboard and dug out a package marked "ration for one".

I read the directions and put it in the micro-oven, setting the timer for thirty seconds. When the buzzer went I fished it out, peeled off the paper cover and found a spoon. I carried the steaming box back to the bench and sat down to eat with the blankets warmly around me.

The soup was blazing hot and seemed to pour energy back into my body, and then there was fish steak surrounded with chopped greens of some kind. In the final compartment in a covered silvery container was a dish of something like ice-cream. That was a neat trick keeping the dessert frozen while the first courses heated.

When I was through I put the empty package in the garbage disposal and looked around. I felt immeasurably better and more alert. Right away I saw the phone on the wall. I don't know how I'd missed it before. All I had to do was pick up the receiver and let Conshelf Ten Control know where I was and they'd have me picked up in no time, and let Jon and Hilary know I was safe. Gosh, there was Uncle Ted and Aunt Janet too! Guiltily I lifted the receiver and waited for the answering voice in Control. I jiggled the holder, wondering what I should say. I realized I didn't know where I was. I'd just have to say I was "here" and leave them to work out where "here" was.

Why didn't someone answer? I jiggled the holder again. It was no good fooling myself. There was the unmistakable lack of noise that meant a broken connection somewhere. I put the receiver back in the wall holder and sat down. I was alone.

For a moment I felt panicky. Then I thought of my rescuer. Of course. That was why he hadn't stayed with me. He'd tried the phone and then gone for help. All I had to do was wait. It was warm, and there was plenty of air, food and water. I settled down on the bench for another nap.

Then someone was shaking me, and it was Jon, dripping wet, still in breather pack and suit.

"Oh, man, am I glad to see you. I still can't believe it. Are you really all right?"

"Fine. I'm just fine." We hugged each other hard. Back on Moon we're not very demonstrative, and I guess at any other time I'd have been embarrassed to death if a guy had done that. But I was so glad to see Jon again! We pounded each other's shoulders and laughed. It had felt so good to be alive, and now I was feeling something more ... how good it was to have a friend who cared. Because it was *me*, not just because I was Moon Governor's son. We stood and grinned at each other like a couple of fools.

"I've got the sled down below with another airpack. Are you okay to travel? Can you manage your suit?"

"I'm great. Really. Go and get the airpack."

He slid down through the exit port and I tidied up the blankets and wriggled into my wetsuit and gear. Jon was back by the time I was ready, and handed me up the fresh air-pack. I gave him my re-breather. His face whitened when he saw the indicator, hard over to zero. He turned the valve to vent the cylinder.

"Not a drop. Oh, man, that was a near thing!"

"You could say that." Then I saw the expression in his eyes. "Hey, I'm all right. I'm here, aren't I?"

"We thought you were really gone. Poor Mum. And your Dad!"

"Father knows?"

"When we couldn't find you within an hour we notified Control. That was around two o'clock. They phoned Uncle George at the U.N. I didn't get the message you were safe till an hour ago. They were trying to get hold of him again when I left."

"Let's go quickly, Jon."

All questions went out of my head. I only wanted to get back to Conshelf Ten and reassure Father. We skimmed back to the habitat, and Jon took me straight over to Control, and introduced me to the operator, Mary. She got me a line to the U.N. I hardly recognized Father on the video, his face was so much older and greyer. But he started to look better right away when he saw me obviously okay and in my right mind.

"Father, I'm so sorry. I wish they hadn't been in such a hurry with the bad news."

"It's all right, son. They had to tell me. After all you only had half an hour's air. How *did* you get to safety?"

"It was the weirdest thing, Father." I paused to wave at Hilary, who had just come into the communications room with a cup of coffee for the operator. "My air was all used up when this strange silver guy with gills suddenly appeared ..."

"Son, I think we're getting a bad line. Would you repeat?"

"This guy—he was covered with silver stuff and he had no ..."

There was a sudden loud bang from the console, a scream from both girls and an acrid smell of burning. The video-phone was dead. I looked up from the blank screen. "What in the world?"

"Hilary, I'm sorry! Did it scald you? I was sure you still had the cup."

"It's all right, Mary, really. But I'll have to change." Hilary was standing by the console, mopping at her slacks. On the floor was a broken cup and a pool of coffee. She saw me staring at her, flushed and went quickly out.

The operator looked up from the smoking console. "I'm terribly sorry, Kepler. I just don't see how it happened. I'm afraid it'll take at least an hour to get this thing dried out and checked over. Do you want me to get your father back as soon as I have a line?"

"Don't bother, Mary. He knows I'm okay and that's all that's important. I don't want to pull him out of conference unless it's urgent."

I bumped into the doctor on my way out of Control. "Oh, Kepler, Jon told me you were safely back. Congratulations! I was just coming to look for you. Come on into Sick Bay."

"But I'm fine, Doctor," I protested, but he strong-armed me anyway, and made me strip down while he checked my lungs and heart, eyes, ears and even my joints.

"Standard procedure," was his only reply to my protests. "Jon told me there wasn't a cubic centimetre of oxygen left in your tanks. How did you time it to the way-station so neatly?"

"I didn't." I told him the whole story, just as I'd tried to tell Father before the console was shortened out. Doctor McIntosh looked concerned and had my head on a pillow and my feet up before I could protest.

"Nitrogen narcosis? ... No way, on that mix. Perhaps an unusual reaction to anoxia. I think we'll keep you here overnight just as a precaution. No, don't fuss, Kepler. A good night's sleep is probably all you need."

I tried to tell him that I'd already slept the whole afternoon away, but I was wasting my time. He brought me a pair of pyjamas, dimmed the light and left me. I tossed about in bed for a couple of hours, and then he came back and gave me a sedative and finally I slept.

I don't often dream. Perhaps it was the sleeping pill. I seemed to hear a woman's voice talking softly, saying the same thing over and over again.

"You didn't see a gillman, Kepler. There *are* no gillmen. You didn't see ..." The voice was low and insistent, and the rhythm of the words seemed to match the rhythm of my heartbeats, and weave themselves into my mind.

When morning came I was given breakfast in bed and then the doctor came. "How do you feel today?" He sat down on the bed. "We're all anxious to know how you got to that way-station yesterday. It's quite a puzzle. It was more than an hour's swim from your position when the current hit. Do you remember?"

"I don't know, Doctor. The more I think about it the more muddled I am. I had such strange dreams.... But I do remember activating the porpoise alarm just before I ran out of air."

"That must be it, then." He got up with a smile. "You seem to be in good shape after your ordeal. But you'd better stay close to the habitat for the next couple of days. No long distance trips, okay?"

"All right, Doctor. What do you mean about a current?"

"Oh, I forgot you wouldn't know. The culprit was a turbidity current. It really shook everything up. Lucky it was so far north, away from the habitat. It's a bit like an avalanche. An instability in the silt deposits from some big river suddenly settles and triggers off an immensely powerful current. Yesterday's was a beauty. It clocked speeds of eighty-five miles an hour before it broke the instruments. Hilary and Jon were lucky. You must have just been on the interface between the current and the ocean. It must have been like riding a roller coaster."

"I wouldn't know! But it was certainly sensational. It threw

66

me into the middle of a kelp bed, and I thought I'd never cut myself out."

"What?" The doctor had walked to the door, but now he turned sharply. "You were actually caught in the kelp? How long for?"

"Hard to guess. I was kind of busy. Maybe fifteen minutes. Why?"

"I don't see how you managed to get to Station 42 on the amount of oxygen you'd have had left, even *with* a porpoise. Well, I don't suppose we'll ever know. The sea is full of mysteries. I'm just glad you made it."

"Me too." I laughed. I didn't add to the doctor's bewilderment by asking how a porpoise could have got me out of my wetsuit and pack and into blankets, nor how it could have operated a resuscitator. I was pretty confused about it myself.

"There *aren't* any gillmen!" I said aloud.

"Well, of course not," Doctor McIntosh said reasonably. "You must have heard some of the rumours and legends and incorporated them into your anoxia hallucination."

"Yes, of course. That must have been it. How did Jon manage to find me so quickly?"

"He was in Control when you phoned and took the message."

"Doctor, I never phoned. The line was out of order."

"Are you sure? Perhaps you were still hallucinating."

I shook my head. "No. Of that I am sure. Check for yourself. Ask Mary."

"I will." He went to the intercom in the passage, and I could hear his voice. He was back in a minute. "You're quite right, Kepler. All the phones in the north sector were taken out by the current. They're still repairing them this morning."

"Odd, isn't it? How Jon found me, I mean."

"Oh, there's some rational explanation. Why don't you ask him?"

"I will, Doctor. I will."

CHAPTER SIX

When I had checked out of Sick Bay I went to look for Jon. He was in class, Mary told me, but I might be able to catch him during coffee-break in an hour. So I wandered over to Marine Biology to visit Uncle Ted and Aunt Janet. They both hugged me, and Aunt Janet kissed me. It was kind of overwhelming.

Up till now I'd considered myself a sort of paying guest in their house, and now it was obvious that they thought of me almost like Jon, like another son. I had to reassure Aunt Janet over and over again that I really was all right. She didn't stop fussing till I threatened to bring the doctor in to swear to my good health and complete recovery.

I knew now how my aunt and uncle felt about me. But what about Jon? What was this cousin thing anyway? Would he confide in me? How would he take it if I pressured him for his own good?

I was beginning to get a weird feeling about this place. On the surface everyone was warm and open, full of the excitement of discovery and a pioneer courage. But, superimposed on this, like a double exposure, was another set of facts, filmy, indeterminate, mysterious. I didn't want Aunt Janet to be hurt by what was going on, if there was anything I could do to help it.

I went back to Central Dome just as the kids were coming out of the lecture rooms. I grabbed Jon and pulled him aside.

"I've got to talk to you alone, Jon. Can you spare a minute?"

"Sure. Let's go into the cafeteria for a soda or something. How are you, Kep?"

"Fine. Just fine." I followed him to an isolated booth in the far corner of the cafeteria. I stirred my milk shake around with a straw and wondered where to start.

"What's on your mind, Kep?"

"A whole bunch of things ... Jon, what do you know about gillmen?"

"Gillmen?" Jon's face was like his mother's—expressive. Fear chased across it followed by the most unnatural blankness. "Gillmen? I don't know what you mean, Kep."

Why did he have to make it so difficult. "Well, you see, Jon, I had this strange dream yesterday, in the way-station, about a gillman rescuing me. Doctor McIntosh says I must have heard the rumours about gillmen and somehow fixed them up into a hallucination. But I'm curious. I don't remember hearing anything about them before yesterday."

Jon mopped up his spilt soda with a paper napkin. "Oh, is that all?" Relief flooded his face. I felt like telling the poor guy that if he was mixed up with a bunch of conspirators he'd better learn to play poker—or get a face mask. "Why, that story's been around for a long time. I guess it's a kind of wish fulfilment. You see, Kep, we're stuck down here in a narrow band of ocean between the surface and about two hundred feet, limited entirely by our physical inability to sustain large pressure changes and to take oxygen out of the water in safe amounts at different depths. So of course the scientists have toyed with the idea of designing a man suitable for life over the whole continental shelf and even the highlands of the Mid-Oceanic Ridge. It would double Earth's living space if it were only feasible. But either surgically or by mutation, it's just a dream. Why, I remember telling you about this idea the very first evening you were down here ... that must be where you got the idea."

"I remember you *starting* to tell me," I put in drily. "But I also remember that Hilary interrupted and wouldn't let you finish. She seemed quite angry. Later that evening you two quarrelled. I wonder why?"

Jon flushed and jumped to his feet. "Hey, look at the time! I've still got three hours of lab work to put in."

"Not now." I put my hand on his arm.

"Don't shout. Everyone's looking at us."

"Then sit down and listen, Jon. I'm not through yet. How did you know which way-station I was at yesterday?"

"I was right there in Control when you phoned in." Jon looked relieved at the change of subject.

"That won't wash. The lines were out on all the phones in the north sector. I couldn't get through. I tried. You can confirm that with Control."

"But I was there, Kep. I got the message," Jon stammered.

"In any case I didn't even know I was in Station 42. I couldn't have given Control the number. Who did? Who knew?"

Jon shook his head. His bewilderment seemed genuine.

"Did you recognize my voice?"

"Oh, no. I didn't take the message myself. I was standing by the console when it came in. Mary took it. She just turned to me and said, 'Kepler's safe. He's in Station 42.' I yelled for her to notify your father and then I grabbed a sled and started out."

"Okay. I'm sorry, Jon. It's all been such a muddle."

"Oh, that's okay." He looked relieved. "About that other thing, Kep. Forget it. There's no such thing as gillmen."

"Darn it, Jon! Now you've got me going again. I've had that phrase running through my mind all morning and it's beginning to bug me!"

We finished our drinks and I went back to Control to bother Mary again. She confirmed Jon's story straight away. "Yes, I had the afternoon shift yesterday. I came on at three o'clock, and the message came through half an hour later."

"Did you recognize the voice?" She shook her head. "You couldn't tell if it were mine or not?"

She laughed. "Oh, I knew it wasn't yours. It was a woman's voice, I'm sure of that. But kind of muffled. I don't think I'd recognize it again. Why?"

"I'm curious as to who notified you of my whereabouts, that's all. I'd like to thank them."

"Why, that *is* strange, now you mention it. I guess we were so glad you were safe we didn't think about it. I wonder why she phoned instead of bringing you in herself?"

"Mary, could you possibly remember where the call came from?"

"Oh, I don't think so, Kep. There was so much going on with Search and Rescue reporting in. I had to relay everything to the Control Map."

"Could you try. It's really important. Suppose you imagine it's yesterday. You're sitting at the console, and you're looking at the board. Now a light flashes. You plug in and a woman's voice tells you I'm safe. Now try, Mary, please."

She sat at the console, frowning with concentration, her hand hovering over the board. "It was up here in the right segment. I remember that ... and it couldn't have been in the top two rows—the forties and fifties were all knocked out by the current." Her right hand reached out experimentally, "Oh, I just don't know, Kepler."

"You're trying too hard. Try with your body instead of your mind. Shut your eyes, Mary, and *feel* it."

She did as I asked and her hand reached up and over, tentatively at first and then surely. "Over there. I remember. One of those two." She opened her eyes and read off the numbers. "38 ... 39. Why, they're both miles away from the kelp beds *and* from Station 42. How odd."

"38. 39. What *is* over there?"

"Mining, mostly. I'll show you on the map. Come over

71

here, Kepler. Look. You were in 42, almost due north of here at the farthest end of the kelp beds. Your previous position was close to 24, to the south of the kelp and a little east. 38 and 39 are over here, on a shelf across a ravine where we did a lot of mineral exploration a couple of years back. Nobody goes near there now."

"Somebody did yesterday."

"Yes." Her face was serious. "Kepler, I'll have to report this to the Controller. He may want Security to look into it."

I didn't want the authorities involved, not till I knew what was going on.

"Isn't that rather a fuss over nothing? I just wanted to clear up the mystery and thank my rescuer. After all, I am safe, thanks to whoever it was."

"You don't understand, Kepler. I saw the map the whole time I was at the console yesterday. There was nobody at all in that sector. That means that somebody must have reported their position falsely and gone over to 38 or 39 secretly. That's really serious. Our mutual safety depends on Control knowing where everyone is all the time. Coming from Moon you must understand that."

"Suppose it was an outsider?"

"Someone from *Topside*? Oh, that just wouldn't be possible."

"Why not?"

"One of *us* would have to be involved. A Topsider would have to live *somewhere*. We'd *know*."

"I suppose so. Well, I guess you'll have to do what you have to. Thanks for your help, Mary."

As I walked back to the cafeteria for lunch I saw Hilary and Jon at a table in the corner. Their heads were close together and Jon was talking hard. Hilary looked up as I walked past with my tray. Her eyes were hard and her curved mouth unsmiling. She looked right past me, and then turned indifferently away.

In the afternoon I suited up and took a three-hour pack out into the habitat. As my weight dropped from me so did my worries. In the clear buoyant water, as I watched the intricately connected lives of the small creatures of the habitat, it became impossible to believe in the reality of that violence I had heard whispered between Hilary and Jon during my first night on Conshelf Ten. I went home tranquil and relaxed.

Aunt Janet had decided that what we needed was a celebration. And she had done us proud. Hilary came to dinner. She was certainly a very different sort of person from Jon. I'd bet *she* could play poker, and her brilliant social mask didn't have a crack in it. It was a beautiful performance. She laughed and told jokes, and never allowed the party to flag for a minute. When she saw I was watching her she gave me a smile that would have melted the Apennine peaks.

It was a fun evening, even though it was half play-acting. Then the phone rang. Aunt Janet answered it, and came back, puzzled.

"That was the doctor, Kepler. He wanted to know if you were still all right, or whether you'd had any more hallucinations. What did he mean by that?"

I tried to laugh it off, but it was embarrassing. I'd been idly playing with the identidisc round my neck, but as my fingers twisted in the chain I must have tugged too hard and it broke. I had no pockets in my sweater or slacks, so I put the chain and disc down on a corner of the table to fix later, and turned to answer Aunt Janet.

"It was just an anoxia dream. The doctor explained it to me. The funny thing is it's still so clear to me, and I have the strange feeling that I've seen the guy before. Which is impossible."

"But one does that in dreams, doesn't one?" Uncle Ted's voice was comfortingly matter-of-fact. "One peoples one's dreams with real people, though they sometimes play unexpected roles."

"I expect that's it."

"I'm sorry if the doctor's message bothered you. Try not to worry, Kepler, dear."

I was sitting at the opposite end of the curved couch from Hilary and as I turned to answer Aunt Janet the lighting caught her face in such a way as to emphasize the slant of her dark eyes, the curve of her mouth. I stared at Hilary, and in the split second that her eyes met mine she knew what I was thinking. I saw the understanding flash across her face, and I knew too that she had seen me see it. My coffee cup slipped and crashed to the floor.

"Oh, Aunt Janet, I'm sorry!" I ran to the kitchen for a cloth.

"I'll find one. Kep doesn't know where you keep things." I felt rather than saw Hilary push past me, and then we were both back in the living room mopping the coffee from Aunt Janet's precious rug.

Hilary's eyes were on me, warning me to say nothing. I ignored her, and opened my mouth to say what I had discovered. At that minute we were deafened by the mechanical howl of a klaxon. The others jumped to their feet and I followed, bewildered.

"Pressure drop!" Uncle Ted's voice was terse. "Jon, take your mother into the living room lock. Hilary, you and Kepler use bedroom one. I'll investigate."

"Oh, Ted, be careful. Oh, my rug, my beautiful rug."

"Quickly, Mother."

"Come on, Kep." Hilary grabbed my hand and ran for the bedroom passage. She climbed up the hoop steps set in the wall, dogged open the hatch and scrambled in with me close behind her.

"Shall I fasten the hatch, Hilary? No water seems to be coming in." I peered down at the floor below.

"When it comes it may come fast. Dog the hatch."

I turned the stiff valve closing, and sat back in the darkness.

Hilary handed me a small breathing mask. "Hold on to this. We've air enough for ten minutes in here, so you needn't put it on yet."

"Don't we have to get out?"

"Not yet. Listen to me, and don't interrupt, Kepler. We don't have much time."

It was the strangest moment of my life, crouched in the tiny air lock in pitch darkness, listening to Hilary's low voice. She moved slightly and her hair brushed against my arm in the darkness. I don't think I had ever felt anything so soft. But her voice was hard, as hard as diamonds.

"Listen, Kepler, and listen hard. For your own good you'd better smarten up and stop poking your nose into things that are none of your business. This isn't your world, and what goes on down here is absolutely none of your concern."

"I thought we'd come to the conclusion earlier that our situation on Moon and yours on Conshelf were rather alike. Why don't you take me into your confidence, Hilary? If I understood what was going on I'd be less inclined to ask awkward questions at the wrong times, wouldn't I?"

"Oh, Kepler. I'm not that naive. I've no intention of telling you anything. Why, even Jon ..." She stopped.

"You mean you don't even trust Jon with whatever it is you know? Hilary, have you thought what that means? If you can't even trust *him*, then whatever it is you know is so bad that he'd be bound to report it, even when it involved you. Hilary, what is it? For goodness sake get out before it's too late."

"I can't ... anyway I don't want to. I'm committed. For Jon it's different. Of course I trust him. But he doesn't have to know, and I don't want to worry him, and ... that's all. It's nothing to do with you. Listen, Kepler. When I first met you I thought you were okay for a Topsider. But I've no intention of allowing you to ruin our plans with your idle curiosity. Be warned. You're meddling in matters far more

75

important than you can imagine. Your life is in danger, Kepler. We don't play games. Stop asking questions. Don't follow me around. Don't badger Jon. And stop asking questions about gillmen. There's no such thing as gillmen, Kepler."

I sat there in the darkness with my mouth open, her last words echoing in my ears. That voice beside me in the darkness of the airlock was the same voice that had whispered in my dreams the night before ...

There was a hammering at the hatch below us, and it was undogged from outside. Cautiously I swung down the ladder. Everything seemed perfectly normal. I followed Uncle Ted back into the living room, Hilary close behind me.

Aunt Janet beamed. "Thank goodness it was a false alarm. My rug!"

Uncle Ted's face was grim. "I'm sorry, Janet. The alarm was genuine. The pressure gauge was sabotaged. If we'd been away, or asleep ... But I got there before there was more than an inch of water on the service dome floor."

"Sabotage!"

"Yes, sabotage. The pressure pump maintains a constant pressure of three atmospheres in our domes, Kepler. This is monitored by a sensitive barometric feed-back circuit. The circuit was jammed. With this." He opened his hand and showed us the silver disc in the palm of his hand. Involuntarily my hand went to my neck before I remembered.

Uncle Ted looked down at the disc and read off the inscription. "Kepler Masterman. 13280. L.L.21." He turned it over and we all looked silently at the engraving of Moon on the reverse. "I'm waiting for your explanation, Kepler."

"Sir, you can't think I had anything to do with it?"

"You don't deny that the disc is yours?"

"No, of course I don't. The chain broke half an hour ago. I put it on the corner of the coffee table."

"Yes, Dad. I remember Kepler doing that."

"Then later you spilt your coffee and went out, ostensibly to get a cloth?"

"That's what I did do, Uncle Ted."

"Did anyone see the disc on the table after you'd left the room?" There was silence. I tried desperately to break through the granite of my uncle's expression.

"Sir, if I were going to do anything so insane as sabotage the pressure unit, would I use anything so incriminating as my own identidisc? I suppose almost anything would have done the job?"

"Oh, yes. Anything flat and about an eighth of an inch thick. A folded piece of cardboard would have done. It's a valid point, Kepler. But if not you ... who? It had to be one of us."

He looked around at Aunt Janet, Jon, Hilary, and then back at me. He made a helpless gesture with his hand, and gave me back my disc. I took it silently and looked on the table and then on the rug for the chain. It was nowhere in the living room. I walked through to the kitchen and looked on the floor there. Nothing.

In the service dome the floor was still wet, and there, gleaming close to the door sill, was my chain. I scooped it up and turned to come face to face with Hilary. She gave me a mocking smile.

"Now perhaps you'll believe me when I tell you not to interfere in our affairs."

"You're mad. You must be mad."

She shrugged and shouldered past me. "I'm late. I'm going home. Goodnight, Kepler. Sweet dreams!"

CHAPTER SEVEN

I saw no more of Hilary. She didn't even come to dinner with us. Jon moped around and was poor company. I wondered if he really knew that Hilary was the saboteur. It was hardly something I could ask the guy, and in not communicating we drifted apart.

I was pretty much on my own during the day, and I spent all my time exploring the habitat. Since the luminous markers radiated a thousand feet from Central I was free of the best part of 300,000 square yards of sea bottom. Even among the constant traffic around the buildings the fish tranquilly lived out their regular pattern of life, and for hours I would lie suspended just above the bottom watching the activities of one particular fish defending its territory, or the antics of the friendly octopus that lived in an overturned canister in the centre of the habitat.

Not that Conshelf Ten was a garbage dump. On the contrary it was as neat as a pin. But the octopus had established squatter's rights to that particular canister when Conshelf Ten was being built, and now nobody would think of moving him. He was a recognized part of the habitat.

After a couple of days of goofing off I asked Uncle Ted what I could do to be useful. On Moon nobody was allowed to be just a passenger, and I felt very uncomfortable bumming around while everyone else was working. So I was appointed chief algae cleaner. It was my job to inspect the outside of the buildings and clean off the algae that would, if left to itself, cover windows, instrument panels and markers with an opaque green film.

It was an easy job. Working three mornings a week I could cover the whole site in ten days, and that was often enough to keep the place shining. I enjoyed the work—it was a change from the computer programming and vector analysis I'd been slogging away at back on Moon. It gave me time to think about all sorts of things I'd never had time for before, while I soared to the top of a dome to polish the high-frequency antenna, or twisted down with an experienced kick of my fins to clean off the observation port of a living unit.

It was wonderful to be free of the drag-down weight of gravity. How could Earth people stand it? The constant energy drain in pulling one foot off the ground, the constant gross weight of one's own body. As I floated weightlessly down from dome top to sea floor my mind seemed to release itself and soar freely. I began to understand much more clearly what Father was trying to do at the U.N. and before the Congressional Committee on Mineral Exploitation.

Compared with the more radical Conshelfers it seemed to me that we Sellenites were not asking very much. We wanted representation as a trading partner at the U.N., and we wanted a freight-cost write-off on all essential goods from Earth. At the moment we didn't own ourselves, the mining companies did.

I remembered again, with bitterness, how they charged us for every ounce of water extracted from the ores in their Lunar processing plants. I found myself comparing the luxuries I'd seen on Earth with the spartan conditions under which we lived on Moon—the monotonous square packages of processed food, the barracks-like quality of our living units, the shortage of books, games, recreation facilities. Moon living was pared down to the bare bones, while the fat cats on Earth got fatter.

There were radicals on Moon who felt that the only answer

was to take over the mining facilities and hold Earth to ransom. But Father and those who supported him knew that that would be a battle in which there would be no winner. Earth could run a blockade that would have us Sellenites on our knees in a week. We were totally dependent on Earth, perched on an inhospitable satellite that offered neither air nor water nor any growing thing.... But on the other hand Earth was becoming yearly more desperate for those rare minerals that were almost exhausted back on Earth.

If Father could get them to make a bargain in good faith, no one would be the loser, and life on Moon would become immeasurably richer. Every night I listened to the news bulletin from Topside, but little was being said. I knew that it was slow, cautious work, that might be ruined at any moment by a hasty move or a too angry word. We had to be patient.

In this new clarity of mind I suddenly realised that if there should be a serious rebellion on the Conshelves it would not only damage the position of moderates like Uncle Ted, the Controllers and most of the other scientists, but that it might wreck the work that Father was doing on behalf of Moon. The first day we had landed on Earth, I remembered, the reporters had tried to draw a parallel between Moon's position and that of the Conshelves.

I decided to get to know the scientists better. I took my lunches and coffee breaks in the cafeteria. I listened and asked questions and poked around.

"If we don't get freedom on our terms, then, Mon, we'll just take it!" the outspoken Scotsman in water control told me.

"There is a certain amount of *talk* about violence," the more cautious Controller allowed. "But there's no chance that it'll come to anything. We all realize that we're far too vulnerable. Topside could wipe us out in a week."

"They couldn't do that," I gasped. "The public outcry ..."

"They wouldn't do it without public opinion on their side.

But if the violence started down here: if some hotheads took over the oilwells or attempted to blockade the foodstuffs we send Topside, then things might easily get serious. Down here we have peaceful cooperative communities. Some of us forget just what it's like Topside these days—the tension, the over-crowding, the desperate need for fuel and food."

"But if they're so dependent on the Conshelves, surely you have the upper hand and can write your own terms?"

"It wouldn't work out that way, Kelper. An animal is only really dangerous when it's cornered. We must give them room to negotiate. If Topside is left with no options they'll destroy us, mark my words. That's why I'm sure there'll be no rebellion."

"Suppose some people down here don't think the way you do, and go ahead against Topside?"

"Then we'd be wiped out."

"Could they do it?"

"Sure."

"Never."

"Now, listen, Mon!" A full-scale argument started up around the cafeteria table. I listened hard. I'd noticed that when people are starting to get a little mad that the unexpected truths start slipping out.

"A land-mine above each Conshelf station and we'd be finished."

"Yeah. Remember the Gulf of Mexico."

"Maybe Topside could mine our positions on the continental shelves, but what about the mid-Oceanic Ridge? They can't bomb that."

"True. But you know full well that living on the Ridge is just a pipe dream. We won't have the capability for years."

"What about the gillers? I've heard tell they've adapted, that they can live down to three hundred feet."

"It's impossible. Man could never adapt!"

"As impossible as a fish learning to breathe air, I suppose?

Aye, and look at the lung-fish, and those crawly beasties in Florida. If fishes can adapt to land, Man can adapt to water. And Man has the surgical know-how and the tools to do it a sight quicker."

"Theoretically maybe, Jock. But I think all this talk of gillers is just that—talk. Unwise talk too. We won't stand a chance of autonomy down here if Topside thinks we're plotting some sort of *coup* behind its back."

"I tell you, Bill, the way the gillers seem to be going is the only way. To cut themselves off completely from Topside, to live independently in the sea. Wake up, Bill. Gillers are a fact of life."

"Oh, pipe down, Jock. You talk too much!"

They pushed their chairs back and the group broke up. I suited up and took an air-pack. I wanted to do some quiet thinking.

Gillers. Gillmen. So they *did* exist outside my imagination, even if they seemed to be in the nature of a very public secret. The doctor had seemed genuinely astonished at my story, but I remembered he'd only been down on Conshelf Ten for a short time. Perhaps he was as ignorant as I had been.

But Hilary was indeed part of the conspiracy, whatever it was, and her lies to me seemed to prove that she must be near the centre of what was going on. She had tried so desperately to make me believe that gillmen didn't exist.

I had to see her again and try to make her understand the danger into which she and her friends were plunging not only the Conshelves, but Moon colony itself.

I swam idly along the bottom, paying no particular attention to where I was going, but keeping in sight a marker tape leading out to the perimeter of the habitat. I tried to think of words to persuade Hilary, to make her change her mind.

I didn't see the sting-ray until I was literally on top of it. It was huge, longer than I was, and about four feet across. There was a flurry of sand, and the tail lashed over like a whip.

Instinctively my hand went up to my face, and I caught the barbed tip full in the centre of my right hand.

The pain was instant and piercing, like red-hot nails being driven into my hand. I writhed on the bottom, holding my hand. I can't move, I thought in panic. But I knew it was going to get worse, not better, and I forced myself to turn and swim slowly back along the marker towards the habitat. My right arm was as heavy as lead. I had to hold it with my left hand, and rely on my legs to kick me slowly along. I was shivering all over, and my knees were beginning to feel like jelly.

It was the middle of the afternoon and the site seemed deserted. I knew I'd never make it without help, but I crawled painfully on. Then at last I saw another diver, the yellow stripe on his suit clearly visible in the blue-green light. His back was towards me, as he checked some instrumentation. I picked up a stone in my left hand, and banged it feebly against a rock in the standard signal for help.

He turned, and came swimming over to me. I showed him my hand. Already it was red and swelling, painfully compressed by the cuff of my wetsuit. My rescuer nodded, patted my arm, and towed me expertly over to Central Dome.

The pain was now so bad that I couldn't even climb out of the water, but huddled against the side of the port, shivering with shock. I could feel hands pulling me out of the water, prying out my mouthpiece and taking off my face-mask. Then I was being carried down the passages to Sick Bay.

Waves of pain surged up my arm and into my shoulder, and getting out of my wetsuit was an agony. Then I was wrapped in heated blankets, while Dr. McIntosh gave me a shot of painkiller, and began to dig the stinger sheaths out of the palm of my hand.

The next few hours were very unpleasant, as my system fought the spreading poison. I was doubled up with cramps and nausea, and shivering with shock. The doctor stayed beside me the whole time, checking my heart and blood pressure, and wrapping my arm in hot towels to ease the pain. Finally the cramps abated, and I fell into an uneasy doze, and later into a deep sleep.

When I woke it was morning. I felt as weak as a baby, and my lips were caked and dry, but the pain was gone. I tried to push myself up in bed, but my right wrist doubled up under me, and I fell back. The doctor got up from the cot across the room and gave me a drink of water. Then he examined me, and smiled.

"You're as strong as a horse, Kepler. No, don't try and move yet. You're fine, but that hand's going to be paralysed for a few days, till the nerves recover."

"When can I get out of here, Doctor?"

"As soon as you can walk across the room without falling flat on your face! Don't worry. A day's rest will take care of the weakness. You've had anti-tetanus shots, and I'll leave you this box of antibiotics, just as a precaution. Four a day till they're finished. Oh, don't look so despondent, Kepler."

"I feel so stupid. I swam right over that sting-ray without seeing it."

"Everyone gets stung by something sooner or later. It's like falling out of a tree and breaking your arm Topside. It goes with the territory. It is unusual for a ray to attack a skin-diver, though. You must have really had it cornered."

"Yes, I guess I must. I certainly didn't mean to."

After the doctor had gone I lay and worried about what I was going to say to Hilary. It didn't seem quite so simple this morning. If I cornered *her*, what would her reaction be?

In the end I got Jon to come and visit me and I asked him to tackle Hilary for me. I told him all the arguments the Controller had given for peaceful negotiation with Topside, and I tried to make it clear how dangerous for Moon negotiations any action or rebellion would be right now.

Poor Jon, he looked thoroughly miserable, especially with

the message I sent at the end. I said, "Be sure to ask Hilary to try and persuade her brother and the other gillmen not to do anything rash. At least give me a chance to talk to her first."

"How did you know her brother ...?"

"It was Hilary's brother who rescued me from the kelp beds, Jon. They are as alike as two peas in a pod, aren't they? You knew all about him, didn't you?"

"Sort of." He looked miserable. "Hilary and I didn't talk about him, about Ian. Not since he went away several years ago. I haven't seen him since."

"Hilary sees him, doesn't she?"

"I don't know. She likes to go off by herself sometimes. I don't know where she goes."

"Will you promise to talk to her. At least give her my messages."

"I don't know, Kep. I don't think interfering will do any good."

"Well, we certainly can't sit by and let the gillmen wreck the whole Conshelf idea, and the Moon negotiations too. Tell her—either she talks to me or I'll tell the Controller and Security everything I know."

He nodded and walked out of Sick Bay. Poor Jon. He should never have got involved with Hilary in the first place. They were too unlike.

I didn't hear a word from Hilary till two days later, and that was just a scribbled note in the familiar handwriting. Mary handed it to me when I went into Central Dome for lunch. It said only: All right. Meet you Map Ref: J10 K7 1400 hours. Come alone.

I pushed the note into the front of my coveralls and went to look at the map. The reference point was immediately south of the big herring corral we'd visited two weeks ago. It was too far for me to swim—I still couldn't use my right hand—so I'd have to requisition a sled. I asked Mary how to go about that, and then hurried into the cafeteria. I'd just have time for a snack before leaving.

It wasn't easy handling the sled one-armed, but by the time I'd left the markers of the habitat behind I'd got the hang of it, though I had to go very slowly. I took a careful compass bearing, and set off, keeping a cautious four feet off the bottom. The previous time I had been on a sled it was as a passenger. Driving the thing was even more exhilarating. There was a sense of speed and power as if I'd suddenly been endowed with the capabilities of a dolphin.

I reached the right reference point with a few minutes to spare. The valve and T-joint were ahead of me, and the silvery bubble wall ran to left and right as far as I could see. By now the corral must be bulging with fat herring ready for the market. As soon as they were netted and taken Topside I knew that the air would be turned off, the pipes dismantled and set up again in another location, and a million or more fingerlings planted to grow to table size.

I parked the sled under the shadow of a big rock about twenty yards from the fence, and I sat on the rock to wait for Hilary. The moments crawled by. Two-ten. Two-fifteen. Perhaps standing me up would be Hilary's way of showing her contempt for my ultimatum. I'd wait till half past two and not a moment longer.

There was a scrape of metal on stone from the rock behind me. I turned and caught a flash of silver out of the shadowy corner of my eye, as a weight came crashing down on the back of my head. In that split second clarity before unconsciousness I thought ... it's the end. I'll lose my mouthpiece and drown. They'll find my body. Fatal accident to inexperienced diver ... then I pitched over into darkness.

I was lying on my back on the sled. My mouthpiece was still firmly in my mouth, held by a silver-covered hand. Its owner was behind me. I whipped up my arm and tried to grab his wrist, but I'd forgotten the sting-ray paralysis. He brushed aside my hand as if it were a strand of seaweed, and was gone in one lithe silvery movement.

I took a few deep breaths, sat up and looked around me. I was boiling with anger. Hilary had indeed shown her hand. I must go straight back to Central and lay the whole story before the Controller. At once, while there was still time.

According to my compass I was facing due north, but where was the bubble fence? Was my compass broken? I turned to the left. To the right. I swam up above the rock and looked all round. The corral had completely vanished. Or had I been unconscious longer that I thought, and had the gillmen moved me and the sled to a position under another rock?

I swam away from the rock, and at once I saw the plastic air-pipe. There was the familiar valve. The perforated pipes ran for miles to left and right, but there was not a bubble to be seen. The air was turned off and the barrier was gone. So were the fish! Three million fish lost. I wondered how many mouths they would have fed, and how much of a loss it would mean to Conshelf Ten.

I swam over to the main air-valve, but there was nothing I could do. I'd better get back to Central and report the loss. I swam towards the sled, and then stopped. Standing by it, one foot on the control bar, was the Herdsman.

I couldn't see the expression on his face, of course. It was hidden by his mouthpiece and mask. But his attitude was very clear. In his hands was a nasty-looking dart-gun, and it was pointing straight at me.

CHAPTER EIGHT

I was formally charged with sabotage and wilful destruction of $1,000,000 of Conshelf Ten property, namely three million prime herring ready for market, and was duly imprisoned.

The jail was not out of the Dark Ages. In fact it was quite comfortable, a suite of bedroom and bathroom, well furnished by Moon standards. But the door was electronically locked and there were TV monitors in both rooms. I had no communication with anyone outside, and there was no telephone, radio or video.

I stayed there for three days while Conshelf Ten prepared for my trial. My jailers weren't rough, but they were unfriendly people. I hadn't got to know the Security forces on Conshelf Ten before. They had their own quarters and didn't eat in the public cafeteria. It was this habit of isolating themselves from the life of the habitat as much as their black uniforms and cold unsmiling faces that put me off.

Security was paid directly by and was immediately responsible to the Topside Government. Automatically it was distrusted. I had noticed that when a Security man walked by, even two women exchanging a recipe for a pie tended to lower their voices or stop talking till he had passed.

Two of my jailers were completely silent. The third, a more angry man, could be induced to talk a little.

"Here, eat this." He'd push a tray of food at me. "And think of all the hungry children you've deprived of a meal. Maybe it'll improve your appetite."

"I didn't do it, you know. I didn't sabotage the corral."

"'Swhat they all say at first."

"I shall go on saying it."

"They all say that too."

"It's the truth. What's the sentence for—for what I'm supposed to have done?"

"Sabotage to the habitat or surrounding environment calculated to endanger the lives of any or all members of the habitat—Death by Dart Gun." He said it with relish.

"The loss of the herring didn't endanger any lives, did it?"

"No, I suppose not." The man sounded regretful. "Sabotage to equipment or property, personal or communal, on or near the habitat, to be punished by a fine equal to the loss sustained by the habitat, plus a prison term of not less than five years and not more than twenty years."

I tried to look unconcerned, but I couldn't sleep that night. There were no books, and I was allowed neither stylo nor paper. I was well-fed, warm, clean, and about to go out of my mind with worry and boredom.

The next morning the Controller came to see me. The stiff formality of his manner and the unsmiling face made me see even more clearly how serious a mess I was in.

"I didn't do it, sir. Please believe me."

He listened to my story, his face expressionless. Then he said, "You are, of course, entitled to Counsel. You may choose any member of Conshelf Ten as your advocate."

"Can't I just hire a lawyer Topside? My father would get me one."

"This is Conshelf business and we handle it ourselves."

"I don't know who to ask—who believes my story."

"Appoint whom you wish. Whoever you choose will plead your case justly. You may count on that."

I wasn't sure I agreed with the Controller, but I shrugged my shoulders. "Then I choose Uncle Ted."

"Edward King, Doctor of Marine Biology, Counsel for the Defence." The Controller wrote in his notebook. "He will be in to discuss your case later in the day."

I gazed at the blank walls for what felt like a week before the door slid silently open and Uncle Ted came in. I jumped to my feet.

"Oh, Uncle Ted. Am I glad to see you!"

He nodded to me, and took a seat across the table from me. "Sit down, Kepler." He drew out a brief-case full of papers. "We have a lot of work to do."

"But ... Uncle Ted!"

"Kepler, my relationship to you now is that of Defence Counsel. I have to tell you that I have seen the Prosecution brief, and they have established knowledge, intent, and presence at the scene of the crime. It doesn't look very good for you. Let me hear everything you have to say."

He heard me through, making notes, and then took me over the whole story again, taping his questions and my answers. When I had finished he shook his head and looked grim.

"But it's the truth. Every word."

"Kepler, the main essence of your defence depends on your unsupported assertion that you were 'set up' by Hilary acting under orders from the gillmen."

"Yes."

"The prosecution will fault you on two counts. Firstly, very little credence will be placed on any attempt by a man on trial to shift the blame to a third party, especially a young lady of Hilary's character and background. Why, she's been known to almost everybody here since she was a child! Secondly, any idea you may have of introducing the gillmen as a red-herring isn't going to work. Who here has ever seen a gillman? Do they even exist? You might as well blame the sabotage on the Loch Ness monster!"

"I want to phone my father!"

"You may speak to him after the trial. You are not permitted to introduce political influence into the process of the Court."

"But he's my *father*!"

"He's also Governor of Moon. You may of course speak to him after the trial."

"Then I want another defence counsel!"

"It won't make any difference, Kepler." Uncle Ted shook his head sadly. "I promise you I'll do my best." He put his papers and recorder back into his brief-case and pressed the door signal. I saw the TV cameras swivel to check my position. He turned back as the door slid open.

"Aunt Janet sends her love," he said softly, and then I was alone again.

I put my head down on the table and cried. I had never felt so alone in my whole life.

After a while I blew my nose and went to wash my face. Anyway, at least one person believed in me still. Maybe I should have picked Aunt Janet as my counsel! I prowled up and down the small room until my legs gave out. Then I lay on the bed and stared at the ceiling.

I lost all sense of time. My watch had been removed with my other personal possessions. An hour, a day, a week ... I ignored the guards and paid no attention to the trays of food they placed on my table at intervals.

Finally the door slid open and two of my three guards appeared.

"Come."

I walked down the echoing passageway, a guard on either side, and along the corridor outside the cafeteria. It too was deserted. Where was everybody? I shivered and the guard tightened his grip on my arm. We stopped at a small door in an unfamiliar passage. One of the guards knocked. The door opened and we went in. I stepped forward, looked up and recoiled against the guards. They grabbed my arms and pushed me forward.

I was standing on the floor of the big amphitheatre in Central. I looked up at the tiers of seats. Every row was filled. Every face was turned silently towards me. I saw Aunt Janet and Jon. His face was white and she was in tears.

The guards prodded me forward to the chair placed centrally on the floor immediately below the lecturer's dais. The silent rows of faces seemed to stare down at me in accusation. For an eternity I stood there, my head up, and stared back.

Then there was a stir, and I turned to see three men enter from the door behind the dais. Each was dressed in black from head to foot. I recognized the Chief of Security as he stepped down to take a seat at my right. After him came Uncle Ted, who moved to a table at my left. Then came the Controller, walking slowly forward to the high carved seat behind the lectern. As the judge seated himself the rows of spectators settled back and one of the guards pushed me down into my chair.

The Controller looked around, and began to speak in a dry, unemotional voice. "Members of Conshelf Ten, we are convened here today in solemn Court of Justice to try Kepler Masterman of Lunar Lab 21, Moon, here present, on the following charge:

"That on August 2nd, 2005, at 14.15 hours he did wilfully and of malice aforethought disconnect by means of a valve the air supply to Corral number Eight, and by so doing cause the loss to Conshelf Ten of approximately three million herring with a market value of one million dollars, and that by so doing the above Kepler Masterman be considered guilty of an Act of Sabotage against the community of Conshelf Ten, as laid out in article 3, subsection 2A, of the Conshelf Criminal Code.

"Kepler Masterman, how do you plead, guilty or not guilty?"

I stood up and faced the accusing eyes of the community that I had so recently began to feel a part of. "Not guilty, my Lord."

"Your plea is noted. I call on Chief Security Officer Jamieson to present the case for Conshelf Ten."

I stood my ground, and faced the Controller. "If you please, my Lord...."

"What is it?"

"Am I not entitled to trial by jury, my Lord?"

The Controller looked up at the packed assembly and then down at me. Was that compassion in his expression?

"This is your jury, Kepler Masterman, the community of Conshelf Ten. We all are your judge and your jury. Now be seated. The trial will begin."

Security Officer Jamieson stood up. "I call upon Colin Terron."

A tall young man, little older than myself, stepped down from among the spectators and up to the witness stand. I didn't remember his face and it wasn't till he began to speak that I realized who he was.

"My name is Colin Terron. I am a Herdsman first class of Conshelf Ten. For the last six weeks I have been in charge of Corral number Eight.... On the afternoon of August 2nd I was patrolling the corral boundary ... I was approaching the southern wall when the air supply to the bubble pipes was suddenly cut off."

"Objection." Uncle Ted was on his feet.

"Will you rephrase your statement, Herdsman Terron. What were you aware of?"

"There was a sudden cessation of bubbles at the perimeter of the corral. The fish instantly began spreading out. I swam at top speed along the southern wall to the connecting pipe and valve.... I saw a diver standing by the valve ... No, I was not at that time able to identify him. Parked under a nearby rock I observed a Conshelf Ten sled, serial number 108.... I commandeered the sled, arrested the diver, and brought him in to Central.... He was there identified as the prisoner, Kepler Masterman."

"Did you subsequently return to the corral, and what did you find there?"

93

"I returned immediately. I found the main air valve to be completely closed. The herring had escaped. The corral was empty."

"Is there any way in which the air valve might have been accidentally closed, perhaps by someone unaware of its function?" Uncle Ted asked.

"It would be completely impossible. It requires considerable physical force to move the wheel that operates the valve."

"In your opinion, that is?"

Colin Terron flushed angrily. "The wheel is approximately 35 centimetres in diameter. It requires a full turn of 360 degrees to seat the valve fully. I am strong and well-accustomed to handling these valves. I find I have to use both hands and exert considerable force to open or close them. It would be completely impossible to open or close such a valve accidentally."

"Thank you ... are there any further questions? ... Mr. Jamieson? ... Then you may stand down, Herdsman Terron."

I recognized the next witness as the man in stores from whom I had requisitioned the sled. I leaned over and whispered to Uncle Ted. He got to his feet.

"My Lord, my client in no way denies his presence at the corral at the time of the alleged sabotage. He was there present. His assertion of innocence is to the act and intent of sabotage."

"Very well. Mr. Jamieson, you will pass on to the next part of your case without calling any further witnesses as to Kepler Masterman's presence at the corral at the critical time."

"Yes, my Lord. I call Janet King to the stand."

Aunt Janet looked tearful and afraid, as if she dreaded what was going to be asked of her.

"You are Janet King, photographer? Will you tell us in your own words what happened on the evening of July 6th?"

"I'm not sure of the date ..."

"The evening of the pressure failure in your living unit."

There was a stir among the listeners, and then an electric silence.

"Oh, that evening. Yes." Aunt Janet looked unhappily across at Uncle Ted and me. "Well, we had dinner ... my husband, my son Jon, his friend Hilary Delaney, and—and Kepler. We were just having coffee when the warning klaxon sounded. We went into the escape locks while Ted investigated."

"What had happened just prior to the warning?"

"Oh ... well, Kepler spilt his coffee."

"And... ?"

"He went into the kitchen for a cloth."

"The kitchen is adjacent to the service dome in your living unit?"

"Yes."

"And the pressure pump assembly is just inside the door connecting the two units?"

"Yes."

"What happened after your husband fixed the pump and you all went back to the living room?"

"My husband ... Ted ... said that the pump had been sabotaged." Aunt Janet whispered the words. There was a stir and mutters from the amphitheatre. The Controller banged his gavel on the desk.

"Can you tell me in what manner it had been sabotaged?"

"Ted showed us a disc which had been pushed under the contact of the barometric feed-back circuit."

"What kind of disc? ... Mrs. King, you must speak up. The jury cannot hear you."

"An identidisc."

"Whose disc? ... I must ask you to speak louder."

"Kepler's. It was Kepler's disc." She burst into tears.

"Thank you." Security Officer Jamieson sat down with a triumphant smile. I found that the palms of my hands were wet. So that was what the prosecution had meant by establishing intent. Hilary had certainly contrived to get me thoroughly damned and discredited. Nothing I said now would be believed.

Uncle Ted got to his feet.

"Janet, when I first showed the disc to Kepler, what was his reaction?"

"He was completely taken aback."

"Did he explain how his disc had got into the circuit?"

"How could he do that? He told us the chain had broken earlier and that he had put the disc down on the edge of the coffee table."

"Did anyone else see him do that?"

"Yes, Jon saw him put the identidisc down on the table."

"Any of us could have picked it up?"

"Yes."

"When the coffee spilt, did Kepler go into the kitchen alone?"

"No. Hilary followed him."

"So she must have seen anything he did?"

"Objection, my Lord."

"Sustained. You are leading the witness into speculation, Dr. King. Stick to the facts."

"I would like to ask a question as to character, my Lord."

"Very well."

"Janet, in your opinion would Kepler Masterman be capable of such an act of sabotage?"

"Oh, no. Absolutely not. He's a quiet boy, not very sociable by our standards, maybe. But he's a good boy, and gentle. Completely unviolent."

"Thank you. No more questions."

"Mr. Jamieson? ... No? ... Then the witness may stand down."

I looked up at the sea of faces. It was obvious that the news of the sabotage to the pressure system in our dome the previous month had surprised and disturbed the Conshelfers.

It had certainly worsened my case. I wondered if Hilary had told the story—how else would it have got out?

Aunt Janet had returned to her seat next to Jon, and was mopping her eyes. She gave me a watery smile and defiantly waved her sodden handkerchief.

I looked for Hilary. Surely her bright hair would be easy to pick out from the crowd. Why hadn't she been called as a witness? I searched the tiers of seats rising to the ceiling of the amphitheatre. She was nowhere there.

I brought my attention back. Uncle Ted had risen to his feet and opened the case for the defence.

"... so, my Lord, although I can call on supportive witnesses to some if not all of my client's statements, in the interests of continuity I will ask Kepler Masterman to take the stand as his own witness, and tell you the whole story of what happened. When the prosecution wishes to challenge him I will produce his witnesses subsequently."

"Very well, Dr. King. You may proceed with your witness."

I walked from the prisoner's chair to the witness stand. I looked up at the amphitheatre full of silent people. I took a deep breath and began my story with my rescue from the kelp bed by one of the gillmen. I described the doctor's reaction to my story and the strange voice I had heard during the night. I told my jury about the mysterious phone call which had led Jon to find me in Way-Station 42, of the woman's voice calling from a supposedly deserted sector. I described how Hilary had spilt the coffee on the communications console while I was describing the gillmen to my father, and I repeated the conversation between me and Hilary in the escape lock, when she had warned me off investigating the gillmen.

I described my conversations with the Conshelf scientists from which I had gradually realized that the gillmen weren't a figment of my imagination. I told the jury how I had realized from the resemblance between Hilary and the gillman who had rescued me that he must be her brother, and that she was deep in the conspiracy. I told them of my ultimatum to Hilary and of her note arranging that I meet her at the corral....

At this point Officer Jamieson jumped to his feet. "Did you in fact meet Hilary Delaney there?"

"No, sir."

"Did you recognize the handwriting as hers?"

"Yes, I think so. I received a note from her once before, Topside."

"Have you still got the message? Can you produce it?"

"No, sir."

"Very well. You may continue."

"I was early. I waited on the big rock near the air pipe ... Yes, the corral fence was still intact at that time. I had been waiting for some time when I was hit on the head from behind."

"Did you see your assailant?"

"No, sir. I only saw a flash of silver."

"*Silver?* You are aware that none of the Conshelf Ten suits are coloured silver? ... Very well. Continue."

"When I became conscious I was lying on the sled. Somebody was holding my mouthpiece in position."

"How convenient! Did you recognize the person?"

"No, sir. He was kneeling behind me. I tried to grab him but he swam away. When I sat up there was no one in sight ... No. I realized almost immediately that the air to the bubble barrier had been shut off, and the corral wall was gone."

"What did you do?"

"I swam towards the valve. I had some idea that perhaps there was something I could do to help. But as soon as I realized that the fish had already escaped I decided to take the sled back to the habitat and inform Control of what had happened."

"And why didn't you?"

"I saw Herdsman Terron pointing a gun at me."

The Controller leaned forward from the judge's chair. "That is your full statement?"

"Yes, my Lord."

"Then, Kepler Masterman, I now require you to swear to the truth of the statements you have just made. Do you swear by Earth or by Moon?"

"I swear by Moon, my Lord."

One of the guards went to the high shelf at the back of the amphitheatre and took down a heavy platinum globe of Moon. My trial was certainly being fairly conducted. They must have had the globe sent down from the U.N. The guard walked back to the centre of the floor, carrying it carefully in both hands.

"Kepler Masterman, you will take the globe in both hands and you will swear that every statement you have made in this court is the truth, the whole truth and nothing but the truth, by the Power that made you, by the Moon that bore you, by the people who nurtured you. Do you so swear?"

As the Controller finished speaking the whole assembly rose silently to its feet. Every face was turned towards me. I stepped forward to the middle of the floor and held out my hands for the globe. The guard carefully placed the platinum model of Moon in my outstretched hands.

AND I DROPPED IT!

There was a concerted gasp from the assembly as the globe slipped through my hands and crashed to the floor. Blushing crimson I bent down to retrieve it. It was much too large to pick up in my left hand, and my right fingers seemed to have no strength in them at all.

"My Lord," I stammered, getting to my feet. "I can't hold the globe. It's too heavy for my hand."

"What kind of evasion is this? Why will you not take the Oath? Dare you not?"

"No, my Lord. I *want* to take the Oath. Every word I've said in this court is true. But my hand—I was stung last week by a ray. My hand is still partly paralysed."

There was a whispering and moving among the members of Conshelf Ten. The Controller hammered on his desk.

"Is Dr. McIntosh present? Please step forward and examine the prisoner's hand ... Is he telling the truth? Is his hand too weak to hold the globe?"

"Yes, my Lord. His right hand is extremely weak. While there is good nervous response the muscle tone is still not restored."

"Thank you, Doctor. Kepler Masterman, you may swear by laying hands on the globe."

The guard picked up the globe. I stepped forward and placed my hands on top of the Moon replica. There was a silence broken by a sudden shout from Uncle Ted.

"My Lord!"

"What *is* it, Dr. King? The case is closed."

"My Lord, before the formal swearing I would like to remind you that additional evidence has just been presented the significance of which may have escaped learned counsel."

"Yes?"

"Kepler, on what day were you hurt by the sting ray?"

"It was ... I think July 30th."

"Three days *before* the sabotage of the corral. What was the state of your hand on August 2nd, when you took the sled to Corral Eight?"

"It was still completely paralysed. I had to steer the sled entirely with my left hand. I remember it was difficult."

"Thank you, Kepler." Uncle Ted turned to the amphitheatre, his eyes sparkling, his cheeks flushed. "My Lord, learned Counsel, members of the jury, you will remember the expert witness of Herdsman Terron to the effect that it required two hands and considerable strength to turn the wheel through 360 degrees and seat the valve in the air pipe. I put it to you that Kepler Masterman, suffering from paralysis in his right hand, was totally incapable of committing this act of sabotage for which he is being tried!"

CHAPTER NINE

There was a moment's stunned silence. Then a roar of
applause, and the whole community of Conshelf Ten surged
forward. The Controller pounded on the desk with his gavel.
Again and again. Slowly the noise died down. The Controller
managed to make his voice heard.

"Members of Conshelf Ten, do you find the prisoner,
Kepler Masterman, guilty or not guilty of the act of sabotage?"

"Not guilty!" It was a single roaring voice.

"And that is the verdict of you all?"

"It is, my Lord."

"Then it is with great pleasure that I now declare Kepler
Masterman to be a free and full citizen of Conshelf Ten."

I was pummelled and pounded and my hand shaken till
it was number than before. Then, caught up in the crowd, I
was swirled along the corridor to the cafeteria, where we had
a party to end all parties. Even Chief Security Officer Jamieson
stopped by to congratulate me. But as he shook my hand his
face was gloomier than ever.

"No hard feelings, I hope, young one?"

"No, sir. None at all. You were doing your job. But how
about you? You don't look so happy to see me free!"

"I'm not." He looked round sourly at the laughing faces.
"Nothing personal, mind you. But what seems to have slipped
everyone's mind is, if you didn't do it, who did? We still have
a saboteur running round loose planning who knows what

mischief. And I and my men have to find him before anything else happens."

"Do you really expect something else?"

"I always expect the worst. You don't get to be Head of Security by believing in sweetness and light and the intrinsic goodness of man. Perhaps that's why I have ulcers." He drained his glass of milk with a grimace and got to his feet.

At that moment Mary's voice came over the intercom. "Controller, please. Urgent."

The Controller moved quickly across the room to one of the wall-phones. "Controller here, Mary."

"I have a call on the line from one of the outlying stations, sir. The caller requests that I broadcast it over the public address system. Do I have your permission?"

The Controller stood, head bent, tapping the phone with his fingernail. "Who is it, Mary?"

"It's a woman, sir. She refused to identify herself."

"Put the call through, Mary."

There was a momentary hissing on the line, and then the voice came through, faint but clear. The laughter and the conversation died down and people sat transfixed, or stood in silent groups, listening.

"Members of Conshelf Ten, we, the gillmen, free men of the ocean, acknowledge responsibility for the so-called sabotage of Corral number Eight. We have issued a manifesto which will be received by the U.N. simultaneously with this message to you. In it we have informed the Topside Government that we Free Men of Ocean demand complete self-government forthwith. Failure to comply with this demand will result in further blockades of those resources which Topside exploits with little or no consideration for the development of the under-sea colonies as independent structures. We, the Men of Ocean, strongly recommend that you of the Conshelves join us in our fight for independence. Our gain is your gain, our goal is your goal.

"However, if you fail to assist us in our fight against Topside we will gain our freedom in spite of you, and your failure to make our cause one with yours will be considered as treachery against the People of the Sea. You too will become our enemy. End message."

There was a click and the hum of an empty line before Mary cut the connection. A roar of excited comment rose from the crowded room. Through it cut the Controller's voice.

"Mary!"

"Sir?"

"Where did the message come from?"

"Way-Station 38, sir."

The Chief Security Officer ran from the room, signalling to his men.

"Mary, get me a line to the U.N. as fast as you can." The Controller turned to face the Conshelfers. His face was drawn. "Members of the Community, I will relay news to you as soon as I get it. In the meantime please keep calm and follow your normal routine as far as possible, unless called upon to render special assistance to Security. Condition Red is in operation from now on until I personally remove it."

I fought my way through the excited crowd to Aunt Janet and Uncle Ted. "Where's Jon? I've got to talk to him."

"He was here a minute ago ... Look, over there. Just going out the door. Oh, Kepler, what is it?"

"Hilary's the key to the whole affair. I'm sure of it. Jon may have some idea where she is. I've got to get hold of her. I'll see you later, Aunt Janet, Uncle Ted." Impulsively I kissed her on the cheek, as if we were saying goodbye. She hugged me, and then let me go. I struggled through the crowd to the door.

The passageway was empty. He could be anywhere. I thought for a moment and then ran into Control to talk to Mary.

"I can't, Kep. It's not allowed."

"Please, Mary. It's life and death, honestly."

"Oh, okay, then." She plugged in a circuit and spoke over the intercom. "Jon King. Calling Jon King. Phone call at Control ... Jon King. Urgent outside call at Control."

It worked beautifully. In about thirty seconds he came panting in. "Where's my call, Mary?"

"Over here, Jon." I stepped out of the shadows. "No, don't run away again. We've got to talk."

"But the phone ... I'm expecting a ..." He stopped short and bit his lip.

"Now who could you possibly get an outside call from? The whole of Conshelf Ten was at the trial, right?" I took his arm and pushed him along. "In fact the only person I haven't seen all day is Hilary. Have *you* seen Hilary? ... No? ... I wonder whether she's planning to phone you. Would it still be from Station 38? ... She'll have to hurry. The Security forces will be out there in a couple of hours. Was that why you wanted to talk to her?"

"What are you doing, Kep? Where are we going? I'm busy. I ... I've got things to do. I can't waste time talking."

"Talking is just what we're going to do. One of these conference rooms seems appropriate. This will do." I shoved him in, locked the door behind me and put the key in the front of my tunic.

"I could fight you for that." He eyed me. "With your weak hand you wouldn't stand a chance."

"That's true, Jon. But all we're going to do is talk. If you're violent it'll just be an admission of your guilt, won't it? Your guilt and Hilary's."

"I've done nothing, Kepler, honestly. Oh, what has happened since you've been down here. Conshelf life was always so wonderful—the trust, the friendship...."

"Was it? I remember the first night I was down here I heard

you and Hilary quarrelling. It had nothing to do with me, and they sounded like pretty basic differences."

He sighed. "You're right. I'm not being fair. Ever since Hilary came back from University Topside she's been different. But she's a beautiful person. You don't really know her, Kep. She wouldn't ..."

"Oh, Jon, do stop kidding yourself! She's slap in the middle of the gillmen conspiracy. I recognized her voice on the phone just now, and if I could, then so did you. She's deep in with them. We've got to find her and try and stop the conspiracy before it's too late. Do you have *any* idea where she is?"

He shook his head. "I wouldn't tell you even if I knew. What do you take me for?"

"An idiot, that's what! Jon, will you stop being noble for five minutes and think. Something bad is going to happen and happen soon. Sabotaging the corral was just a preview to the main event. You won't help Hilary by protecting her."

"I don't believe they're going to do anything serious. I think the whole thing's a bluff."

"I suppose setting me up and letting me be sentenced to ten to twenty years was just a bluff too. Hilary couldn't have known that my hand would turn out to be my alibi. Come *on*, Jon. She's ruthless."

Jon stood irresolute. The intercom crackled and burst into urgent words.

"Attention all personnel. Attention all personnel. This is Security. The loss of four kilos of high explosives has just been reported from the geophysics lab. Repeat. The loss of four kilos of high explosives has been reported. Any person able to give information is asked to call Security immediately. The following personnel from Geophysics will please come to the Security Office ... Baker ... Jones ... Philips...."

I looked across the little room at Jon. "*Now* will you believe that they're not playing games?"

Jon slumped down at the table and put his head in his hands. He gave a shaky sigh.

"I always knew she was committed all the way. I just kept hoping ... It's not her fault, Kep. It's her brother's influence. They were always very close. She'll do anything for him."

"Okay, Jon. You really want to help Hilary? Then you've got to help me find her before Security does, and before any more damage is done."

"But I don't have any idea ..."

"Listen. There has to be a logical place. You've lived in this habitat almost all your life. You know all the possibilities."

"She can't be in the habitat. Security will have searched everywhere by now."

"Okay. And she can't stay in the water for ever. Surely that means that she's hiding out in a way-station."

"Kepler, there are over fifty of them."

"Let's think. The phone calls came from Station 38 both times. A woman's voice, it must have been Hilary's, both times...."

"Security went straight there. We can't help her if she's still there."

"She won't be. I have a hunch that she never was! Listen, Jon. There's something odd about both those calls. The timing is crazy. Half an hour after I was acquitted the phone call came acknowledging the gillers' responsibility for the sabotage of the corral. How far is Station 38? ... Fifteen miles? How did they find out the result of the trial so fast? Is there any way of communicating between stations?"

"Not without going through Control switchboard."

"And Mary swore there were no other calls either in or out, during and after the trial. I checked that with her. Now remember the first call. I was in Station 42, and the message that I was safe came from Station 38 around 3.30. How? My rescuer couldn't have swum out there to make the call. And in any case it was Hilary's voice."

I paced up and down the small room. It didn't make sense. There wasn't enough *time*. Suddenly I got it.

"Jon! Tell me exactly what you and Hilary did from the time we got separated in the kelp beds until the phone call. Were you together all the time?"

"Yes, I mean no. Sorry. I mean we swam together through the kelp beds, separating to left and right to cover the ground faster. We kept in touch on our intercom."

"You could hear her the whole time?"

"Yes, definitely. Then our air ran low and we went back to the sled for the new packs. We knew then that your air would be gone too. That there was no good searching ... Gosh, Kep, that was the most awful part. We were sure there wasn't any hope, but we felt we couldn't go back without you. So we took the sled and made a complete circuit of the kelp beds."

"You must have passed pretty close to Station 42."

"Yes, I suppose so. But we weren't thinking of way-stations just then. We were looking for you—your body—in the kelp."

"Did anything unusual happen? Did you see anything? Stop for anything?"

"Yes. On the southern leg of our circuit—when we were just turning back to the habitat actually, Hilary had me stop the sled. She thought she saw something under a rock."

"Did you see anything?"

"I thought I saw a flash of something white or silvery. I can't be sure. Anyway I stayed with the sled and Hilary swam over to investigate."

"And?"

"She said it was just a dead fish."

"Was she gone long?"

"Maybe five minutes."

"Could you see her the whole time?"

"Not every minute. She swam back behind the rock."

"Then you took the sled back to Central and got the search and rescue started?"

"Yes.'

"Was Hilary with you the whole time?"

"On and off. We showered and changed. Then we stayed in Control, by the map. It's strange—I remember now. Hilary looked kind of odd."

"Scared? Upset?"

"No. I remember being surprised. I was feeling shivery and kind of sick. I looked across at her and her cheeks were flushed and her eyes sort of dazzly. You know the way she looks?"

"Yeah. I know. What happened then?"

"Then she suddenly said, 'I've got to get out. The suspense is killing me. I'll see you, Jon.' Something like that."

"What time was that?"

"I don't remember."

"Come *on*, Jon! Try. Relate it to something else that was going on. Did you look at your watch around then?"

"No. I didn't. But Mary came in to relieve Terry at the switchboard. It was right then."

"Three o'clock." I remembered. "Jon, that's exactly half an hour before the phone call. Come on. Let's go and look at the map."

I unlocked the door and we raced back to Control, and over to the wall-sized map.

Jon arced his finger around the habitat. "Four knots is about max for these sleds. And Hilary had to suit up. She couldn't possibly have got farther than this."

"That isn't much. Only two way-stations. Would they be busy ones?"

"Oh, sure. The biologists use these ones all the time. They're doing a lot of work around there, and it's just too far to get back to the habitat for coffee breaks and meals and so on. Yes, they'd be really busy."

"And Hilary would know that, of course? ... Is that all?"

"I'm afraid so."

"What's this?" I pointed at a small black square about a mile and a half from the habitat.

"Oh, that's just an old storage unit. It's not even active now. That's why it's marked black on the map. There's no galley or showers. Just a bunch of shelves."

"Would it have a phone?"

"Sure. But it would be disconnected at the switchboard."

"So much the better, if my hunch is right. Look, Jon. We know that it's physically impossible for Hilary or anyone else from the habitat to have got up to Station 38 in time to make either of those phone calls. Okay? So it didn't happen!"

"But ..."

"Suppose the gillmen have been planning their conspiracy for a long time. They'd have to have information from someone in the habitat—someone nobody'd suspect. Hilary. Her brother is a gillman. Things started happening as soon as I came down to Conshelf Ten. I've been puzzling why. But *Hilary* came back to the Conshelf the same time I did. That's why things started happening. They needed Hilary before they could start.

"Now suppose they connected the phone in the storage unit to the phone in Station 38, then Hilary could send messages from close to the habitat to the deserted area near the mines. I bet that's where the gillmen live—in the deep water near the old mines. And when Hilary phoned those messages to Control, she was phoning from the storage unit, but the switchboard indicated that the call came from 38. It made a perfect built-in alibi."

"You think Hilary is still hiding in the storage unit?"

"Can you think of a likelier place?"

Jon shook his head miserably. "What are you going to do, Kep? Tell Security?"

"Of course not. I told you. We're going to have one last

try at making Hilary and the gillmen see reason. Against Security's dart-guns there'd be a showdown and nobody'd win. Let's go and suit up."

As we crossed Control Mary called out. "Kep!"

I turned, suddenly afraid.

"Sorry. I didn't mean to startle you. The Controller has just heard that your father is due to make his formal presentation in the General Assembly of the U.N. early tomorrow. We'll keep the TV tuned in for his speech and the voting. Good luck."

"Thank you, Mary." I went to suit up with my head spinning. The time for Father's presentation of Moon's case must have been put forward. It was much sooner than we'd expected. I wondered who was responsible for cramming it through, and why. I knew it couldn't be Father. Hurry just wasn't his style.

I stopped suddenly in the middle of struggling into my wetsuit.

"What's the matter, Kep?"

"The explosives! The gillmen wouldn't take them till they were ready to use them. They must be going to make their move very soon. If they do something violent before the U.N. vote is in, Moon's case will be ruined."

I don't think Jon really understood. His whole mind was in a fret over Hilary.

"Kep, who took the explosives?"

"It had to be Hilary. You know that. Probably when every one else was at the trial."

We checked each other's suits and were sitting on the edge of the exit port when Jon exclaimed.

"Security!"

"What about it?"

"Condition Red. I'd forgotten. We can't leave the habitat without permission. And there's no way we can get a sled."

"Then we'll go without one. Can you get us out of the habitat without being seen?"

"I guess so. Yes, sure. Stay close."

We swam in the shadow of the buildings till we came to the perimeter. We could see the vague figures of the guards patrolling the habitat, guns at the ready. I remembered the former peace and tranquillity of Conshelf Ten, and I felt very angry.

We lurked under a living dome until the bubbles of an incoming sled momentarily obscured the water. Then we swam fast and silently out of the habitat.

My legs were aching and my right arm was numb by the time the small dome of the storage unit loomed out of the blue-green haze.

We swam closer and I held Jon back from the entry port, put my fingers to my lips and shook my head. I began to swim slowly round the dome a few inches off the bottom.

Half-way round I found what I was looking for—a line already grey-green with algae which snaked off from the hut in a north-easterly direction. There was our phone cable to Station 38 all right.

Was anyone inside the hut? I swam to the side of the hemisphere and hung against the curved side, my head against the metal wall. I tried to quiet my breathing.

What was that? I waited. It came again, the unmistakable scrape of metal on metal. Someone was moving around inside. Would it be Hilary. Or someone else?

One of the problems of underwater entry was that for the few seconds of surfacing and getting rid of one's face-mask one was entirely blind and vulnerable. Somebody could hit me on the head as I surfaced and that would be the end of that.

I beckoned Jon away from the hut. "Jon, I'm going in. I'll have one last try at talking sense into Hilary. I want you to go back to Central. If I'm not back in an hour, or if I haven't phoned to say I'm okay, tell Security the whole story—everything, Jon. Okay?"

"Let me come too."

"No way, Jon. You're my insurance. If I do phone I'll use your name just once if everything is all right. But if I'm being forced to call then I'll keep repeating your name. That means to forget everything in the sentence I use your name in. Got it?"

"Yeah. Like Simon Says." He put his hands on my shoulders. I could feel the pressure right through my heavy suit. Then he turned and began to swim back to the habitat.

I waited until he was out of sight and then ducked under the dome. I came up without a splash, my hand ready to rip the mask off my face the second I cleared the surface of the water.

CHAPTER TEN

It worked perfectly. Hilary had pulled out a couple of shelves, and was lying on the uncomfortably narrow bed left by the gap. I was on the floor and getting out of my airpack before she could get to her feet.

"What are you doing here? How did you find me?" Her cheeks were paper white, her eyes dark with fear.

"It wasn't too hard to work out. Hilary, I want to help you. I mean you no harm, honestly. But we must talk."

"You mean *me* no harm! Do you know what danger *you've* put yourself in by coming here? Oh, Kepler, please go away and pretend you never saw me!"

"I can't do that."

"Sure you can. Did anyone see you come? Well, then ... No, wait. You couldn't have found this place by yourself ... Somebody brought you, didn't they? Was it Jon? Is he out there?" She bent over the exit port, gazing anxiously down into the water. "Go back, both of you. Please. Before it's too late."

"I'm alone, Hilary. Jon brought me, but he's gone back to the habitat."

"To tell Security, I suppose, while you keep me here!" She sprang at me, but I managed to pull her wrists down to her sides.

"No, no, no! Hilary, *will* you listen. We have an hour to talk before Jon tells Security everything we know about you and the gillmen. An hour for you to think, and change your mind. Hilary, you can't want to destroy everything that Conshelf life stands for? Everything your father helped make possible?"

"Of course I don't. It's the opposite. We have to join the gillmen in their fight against Topside. We'll get our freedom."

"But the Conshelfers don't like what you're doing. They don't *believe* in what you're doing. Of course all the Conshelfers want independence and a square deal in the market place. But there's only one possible way to achieve that, and it's not through violence. It's not by pushing the Topside Government up against a wall. Not by depriving innocent thousands of people of food and fuel. No way!"

"We differ. I guess we'll always differ, Kep. My father and one of my brothers and all their friends died in the Gulf of Mexico because we relied on reason and negotiation."

"Then stop talking to the Government and talk to the people. Make *them* aware of your problems. Persuade *them* to pressure the Government to give you a fair deal—through votes and the pressure of public opinion. Do what my father's doing—appeal to the U.N. Sure we could use violence on Moon too. But nobody wins that sort of deal. We'd all suffer."

She shook her head. "Tell me that again when your father walks out of the General Assembly with the vote for an independent Moon in his pocket. Then maybe I'll believe you. It's no good, Kepler. We're committed. We can't turn back. Go back to Conshelf Ten, Kepler. Forget you ever saw me. It's your last chance."

"I'm sorry, Hilary. But you see, I'm committed too."

"That's it, then. Stalemate." She smiled a small sad smile. Her eyes moved slightly, looked over my shoulder. I turned, but I was too late. The blow came down on the back of my head. My knees buckled and the light went out....

When I opened my eyes the lights were flickering on the circle of water in a dazzle of colour. I shut my eyes again.

Ouch, my head hurt! I moved and tried to sit up.

I was lying on my side by the exit port, looking down into the water. I could feel the weight of my airpack against my shoulders. My wrists were tightly tied in front of me, and my knees and ankles were bound too.

Hilary knelt down beside me. "I'm sorry, Kep. Do you feel awful? We're getting out of here." She slipped my mouth-piece in for me, and pulled down my face-mask. "Okay?"

I nodded, and then wished I hadn't. I thought my head was going to fall off. Carefully Hilary rolled me over till my legs were in the water, and then she eased me down, holding my mask on with one hand. Strong hands pulled me from below. Like a parcel I was passed from hand to hand, and finally tied, flat on my back, to a sled lying on the bottom near the dome. I looked up into the shadows and saw Hilary slide down through the port.

The sled stirred and gathered speed. In spite of my fear I couldn't help a surge of pure excitement at the sight of my escort. There must have been fifteen gillmen around the sled. They moved with a graceful economy of motion, flashing through the water like a school of mackerel, silvery, free, totally at one with the water. Almost I envied them.

We travelled fast. I had no idea of the direction, and there were no landmarks for my unaccustomed eyes. It seemed many hours before we came to the end of our strange journey, though it must have been less than three, since my air was still okay.

Quite suddenly the water was full of gillmen, silver bodies flashing around me on all sides. I was lifted off the sled and carried through the water, and pushed up into a dome. Unseen hands untied my arms and legs, removed my face-mask and airpack. Then I was alone.

I lay for a long time face down on the floor, tired and nauseated. When the pounding in my head eased off I sat up and looked about me.

I was in the strangest room I had ever seen. It was like a

bubble, a sphere of glass and plastic, totally transparent. Sitting at the bottom of this flimsy globe I felt deeply insecure, the whole weight of the ocean pressing in on me from all sides. I was to find that for the next night and day I would be seized, in unguarded moments, by a sudden feeling of falling, and I would jerk and fling out my arms in an involuntary effort to save myself.

There was neither furniture nor machinery in my bubble, and I couldn't understand how the air remained fresh and the pressure constant. The gillmen had obviously developed skills for underwater living far beyond the technology of the Conshelfers. I found my prison uncomfortably damp and cool, though, and I kept my wetsuit on for warmth.

At first I couldn't understand why my arms and legs had been untied, and why there appeared to be no guards. But when I looked at the dark ocean around me and realized that there was no breathing pack in the bubble I understood why no bars or bonds were necessary. It must have been the most efficient jail on Earth.

When Hilary appeared with a meal for me after a few hours she confirmed my suspicions.

"We're nearly a hundred feet below the surface here, Kepler. It would take thirty-six hours to decompress safely once you're saturated. You have no breathing unit, and any attempt to make straight for the surface would result in certain death."

"Hilary, how could you do this?"

"I had no choice. Our plans are finalized. Already the high explosives we took have been planted on all the oil rigs along the East Coast. Tomorrow we give the Topside Government our ultimatum. You were in the way, Kepler. I'm sorry, but this is war, and we can't afford to be sentimental about it."

"I wish I could talk some sense into you. The gillmen—the ones who are really holding me here—can I talk to one of them?"

"It's very difficult. They can't stay in air for long, or their gills dry out. Talking in air is a problem too. You see their lungs are filled with fluid when they make the switch to gill-breathing. They use different ways of talking, ways you couldn't understand."

"They've really committed themselves to the ocean, then?"

"Yes, Kepler. There's no turning back for them. They've given their bodies to ocean living, so you see the ocean *must* belong to them."

"What was done to them—it's not reversible at all?"

"We don't know. It hasn't been tried."

"And the red-haired guy who rescued me from the kelp-bed is your brother, isn't he?"

"Yes. I knew you'd caught the resemblance that evening at the Kings'. That's why I sabotaged the pressure pump. Oh, Kepler, I warned you and warned you. You wouldn't leave it alone. So I had to set you up for the sabotage of the fish corral. I hoped they'd keep you in jail till the rebellion was over. I'd have told Security the truth as soon as I could, honestly. I'd no intention of letting you go to jail for ten years, really, Kep."

"Thanks," I said drily. I looked curiously at Hilary. She was lounging on the transparent floor of the bubble, looking like the cover-girl off some futuristic fashion-mag. Yet she was talking so lightly of war and sabotage. I was angry and I tried to hit back.

"How come you didn't take the plunge and become a giller like your brother if you think their cause is so wonderful?" It got to her. I saw the warm flush flood her pale skin. She bit her lip.

"I couldn't stand the idea of being mutilated. It gave me the horrors. And suppose the operation is irreversible. I'd have lost Jon. I could never be with him again."

"You couldn't persuade him...?"

"Never. He's the logical law-abiding type. So solid and

secure. Perhaps that's why I loved him. Like you, Kepler. Like your father. When I first met you I thought *you'd* understand what we were fighting for. Your Moon situation is so like ours. You're treated like ore-producing robots. But you disappointed me. What does your father do? He comes to Earth and asks pretty-please! Asks! He should be demanding."

"Hilary, what would you do if you were swimming along and in a corner of a rock-face you met a tiger-shark head on? Would you back it still further into the corner? Maybe punch it on the nose?"

"Of course not. You'd get out fast and give it a chance to get away. Oh, I know what you're really saying. But humans aren't like animals. They're a darn sight less rational, if you ask me. If you give them any quarter they'll take advantage of you."

"Oh, Hilary, you're wrong. Why are you so cynical?"

"You want to know? Okay, then. My Dad was Safety Officer on the Gulf Conshelf. Ian was just a little kid then, but he didn't forget what happened, and he told me. Dad begged and begged Topside to go for separate life-support systems in the domes. But they wouldn't buy it. Company profits were more important than the life of the men and women on the Conshelf.

"When the earthquake struck, fifteen of them were killed instantly, and twenty-three were crippled for life. Dad didn't die for a principle. He didn't die for his country. He died because he was stupid and *asked* for safe living conditions when he should have demanded them."

She looked so beautiful with her dark eyes filled with tears, her red hair flowing over her shoulders, that my heart pounded uncomfortably in my chest. I tried to concentrate on ways of getting past her anger.

"I know the story, Hilary. I'm sorry. But I disagree with your verdict. I believe your father did die for a principle:

for the principle that in the long run it is better to negotiate without anger than it is to force issues through violence.

"It was a terrible price to pay, but think, Hilary. No one Topside today would ever argue the fact than all Conshelf units must have separate life-support systems, however costly. If your father had forced their hand they might have given in grudgingly, but always with the underlying feeling that at some time in the future they might reverse their decision. Lasting changes cannot be forced, Hilary. They must arise out of the desire of people for what is right and best. But, oh, it sometimes takes so long...."

She got up and prowled up and down the bubble. "Oh, Kep! It's so idealistic, it's beautiful. But it won't work. Look. Tomorrow is your father's speech before the General Assembly ... oh, don't look so surprised! We have our ways of keeping in touch with what's going on. Suppose the U.N. votes to leave Moon in the hands of the mining conglomerates, what do you do then? Go home and slave for another fifty years?"

"It isn't going to be like that, Hilary. We have justice on our side. I know Father will get the vote." I tried to make my voice sound convincing.

"You don't know the power of the lobbies down here. Even your father. He may be Moon Governor, but down here he's just an innocent. You all are!"

"We're not completely naive. We have considered the possibility of failure. We've even made plans to cover that possibility."

"Non-violent plans?"

"Certainly."

"Well, tell me."

"Hilary, I can't. It's top secret."

"Sure." She shrugged and turned away. I looked at her stiff back, with the red hair flowing like fire down it. I bit my lip and prayed that I was making the right choice. I knew instinctively that in this one girl was the key to the whole giller rebellion.

"Hilary, if I tell you our plan will you promise solemnly to tell no one, not your brother, not Jon, no one...?"

"I promise."

"This place ... it's safe?"

"You mean, is it bugged? Of course not. You may be a prisoner, but we wouldn't spy on you or trick you." She flushed angrily.

"Okay. Come close. I can't say it aloud."

It was terrible to be talking of things to which I was sworn, but more was at stake than either my father or the Moon elders could ever have dreamed.

"For the last six months we have been secretly rationing our water supply, and storing all we can spare deep in Moon. If the U.N. abandons us to the mining companies again, and if Father can get no promise of better living conditions from their Head Offices here on Earth, then when we get back to Moon we will refuse to buy any more water from them. We'll ask them to give it us free. If they refuse we'll do without. The children and anyone who's sick will get regular rations from our secret supply. The rest of us will do without."

"But you'll die!"

"That's hardly likely. Our action will be made known on Earth. In fact it's all been arranged just in case there should happen to be an unfortunate break in communications at the critical time. You see, we're not that naive. Twenty-four hours after Father and I return to Moon, all Earth news media will have the full details of our ultimatum. Of course, if the companies are obstinate we'll get sick pretty soon and be unable to work. It won't be a strike. We'll really be sick. We'll take special precautions to make sure there's no damage to company machinery. The responsibility will be all theirs."

"It's magnificent." Hilary's eyes shone. "It's such a gesture. Like dumping the tea in Boston Harbour. Only more so. The colonists could live without tea. You can't live without water."

"That's why I'm so sure we'll get justice. Do you see, Hilary, how much better it is? If we blew up the mine installations they'd have every right to bring us to our knees, and they'd have the sympathy of Earth in doing it. We'd be worse off than we are now.

"The same thing is going to happen if your gillmen blow up the oil rigs. Topside will retaliate with the full power of public opinion behind it."

"It's not quite the same, Kep. Topside can't touch the gillers. That's why their development has been kept secret all this time. The gillmen are self-sufficient. They don't need fresh water or air. They have the whole mid-Oceanic Ridge for a home, and all the natural and mineral resources of the ocean at their disposal. Topside can't touch them."

"Maybe not. But they can sure touch the Conshelfers. They can cut off communications, fresh water, even air, I suppose. The whole undersea programme would be ruined. Would the gillmen be better off then? What would they gain by turning their backs on mankind, and mutilating their bodies to live in the ocean? Loneliness. Isolation. That's what. If they were cut off completely from the rest of the world of men, I think that pretty soon they wouldn't *be* men any more.

"Dolphins seem to have bigger brains than Man, and they can communicate with each other. But what have they achieved in terms of social or technical development compared with men? You were wise not to become a giller with Ian, Hilary. He and the other gillmen are out on a limb of the tree of evolution, and they're just about to saw off the branch!"

Hilary burst into tears. I drew a shaky breath and looked cautiously at my watch. It was almost midnight. Tomorrow Father would make his speech. Tomorrow the gillmen would give Topside their ultimatum. In about twelve hours it would all be over, one way or the other.

Had they told Father I was missing? I hoped not. Nothing should distract him from the job he had to do, for the sake of all us Sellenites, and maybe for the sake of the gillmen and the Conshelfers too.

"I'll go and talk to Ian, Kepler, at once. Maybe there's still time. But you must let me tell him your plan, Kep, you must. There's no other way I can persuade them not to go ahead and blow up the oil-rigs. Please!"

"I can't. Not possibly. I should never even have told you. You've got to persuade them your way, Hilary, with your ideas. You mustn't even hint at the Sellenite plans."

"I can't." Her voice was flat with despair. "They won't listen, I know. And our beautiful life down here will be ruined for ever. Oh, Kep, why didn't I listen to you before?"

"It didn't make any sense to you before. If it had then you would have listened. Look, could you at least persuade your brother to wait until the results of the U.N. vote are in? Don't ruin Moon's chances. You know what it'll mean to us. If the U.N. vote is in favour of Moon's independence, then you know that your gillmen too will stand a fair chance in the world court. Will you try and persuade Ian at least to wait?"

"If that's all I can do, I will." Hilary stood up and I helped her strap on her tank and check the valves. She sat on the edge of the exit port and pulled down her face-mask.

"Goodbye, Kep."

She put in her mouthpiece and slid through the exit of my prison. She turned outside in a silver swirl of bubbles and waved. Then she vanished into the greenish gloom of the sea, and I sat down again on the transparent floor to wait.

CHAPTER ELEVEN

How did I pass that long night? I lay in the darkness of my bubble prison, and I played back in my mind everything that had happened to me since I had come to Earth. I went further back, through the fifteen years of my life on Moon.

A strange thing happened to me. I realized how much I loved my life under the sea, and in contrast how lonely had been my childhood on Moon. I had been the firstborn child, and the son of the Governor. These accidents of birth had left me in an isolated position I had never been able to break out of. Climbing mountain peaks is great—but where's the challenge when you've been born on one?

I tasted the thought of how my life might change if I stayed with the Conshelfers—maybe married to a gorgeous intelligent girl like Hilary. Then I started thinking of Ann back on Moon, and I felt horribly guilty, which she'd have hated.

Was that the dawn, that faint change in the gloom of the water? Or just my eyes adapting. I could see the luminous dial of my watch—six o'clock. Topside the world would be stirring for the start of another day; people would be throwing open their windows, yawning, breathing in the free, fresh air.

I began to feel I was suffocating in my plastic prison. How many atmospheres of pressure did the weight of water above me exert? Hilary had said we were a hundred feet down. It seemed a frightening depth, three atmospheres of water, plus the weight of the air itself on the surface of the water—four atmospheres!

I suppose Earth people felt ill at ease on Moon, with airless space ready to snatch and dissipate any unprotected liquids or gases, but to me it was commonplace, and associated with lack of pressure to me was the life of low-grav.

In this bubble I was doubly prisoned, weighted down by gravity and threatened by the enormous pressures of the deep. I lay on the floor of the bubble, with the sweat streaming off me. There was no escape....

I lay and tried to keep my sanity by picturing the windless cloudless Moon skies, where the stars of the Galaxy burned down with the brilliance of a million diamonds. That was where Ann was. That was where I belonged. I clenched my fists and lay on the bubble floor, willing time to pass.

A noise startled me and I sat up. Hilary at last! I went over to help her in. When she pushed back her face-mask I knew by the expression in her eyes that she hadn't been successful.

"Didn't they buy any of it?"

She shook her head sadly. "If you'd only let me tell them your Moon plans...."

"I couldn't."

"I know, Kep. They heard me out. But it was like an exercise in political science—just theory. Very interesting, but not where they're at. They're desperate men, Kep. Sometimes even Ian ..." She shivered. "Since I came back from University Topside, he's changed. He seems so cold, so alien. I can't reach out to him any more. I love him, but ... but he's not really my big brother any more. He's changed into something else."

I put my arms around her. "Don't. Maybe there's still a chance."

She sniffed. "I'm okay, really. Anyway they did promise they'd hold off their manifesto until your father's speech is over and the vote's in. Ian did understand that they might ruin your chances if they struck this morning. But it still gives us only a few hours respite."

"A lot can happen in a few hours. We mustn't stop hoping." I looked at the waterproof bag lying beside Hilary's air-pack and mask. "What's in the package?"

"Oh, yes. I got some sandwiches and a water flask. And I brought you a radio. Your father's speech starts in an hour."

"Thank you. It's so important...."

"You don't know how important. I said that Ian and the other gillers will wait till the vote is in before going ahead with their rebellion. Ian said, right at the last, that if the vote was overwhelmingly in Moon's favour, they just might reconsider their plans."

She looked across at me, hope in her eyes. I bit my lip.

"It's terrific, Hilary. Only ... well, Father never expected an overwhelming vote. It would be almost too much to hope for."

"I thought that was how it would be. Ian smiled at me, in such a way, with his face all twisted." She sighed, and got to her feet. "I can't stay, Kepler. I hope it isn't too lonely for you here."

"Hilary, please give me your airpack. Give me a chance to get out of here."

"I can't, Kep. You know I can't."

"I could take them from you."

"I doubt it, with your weak hand. And I studied judo Topside. I can't let you go. You wouldn't stand a chance, you see. We're twenty miles from Conshelf Ten. You'd never make it without a sled, even if you knew the direction."

"And what if I went up? If I took the full three hours?"

"A hundred feet? It'd take about thirty-six hours to decompress safely. I'm sorry, Kep. You really are a prisoner."

"Almost as much as Ian and the other gillmen."

Her face twisted. "Yes, almost as much as them."

I stood by the exit port and looked across at her. I could feel the determination to break out of this bind growing in me like a great force.

"Listen, Hilary, before you go. The gillers are more prisoners than I am. We're both prisoners of our environment. But *they* are prisoners of their anger too. It's made them blind. If they resort to violence they'll kill the whole beautiful undersea dream that they've sacrificed themselves for. Tell them that, Hilary. Try to make them see past their anger to the reality."

She looked up at me, her slanting dark blue eyes clouded. "I'll tell them, Kep. But it won't change anything."

She pushed down her face-mask, replaced her mouthpiece, and slid off the edge of the bubble into the dark water. I saw the glimmer of her suit, and then I was alone once more. I looked at my watch, turned on the radio softly, and ate the breakfast Hilary had left me.

The sound of my father's voice jerked me back from an uneasy doze. How strange it was to hear his familiar voice in this alien place. I swallowed, blinked my eyes, and concentrated on what he was saying. Or rather, since I knew what he would be saying, I concentrated on the response he was getting. I wished I had a video set. The clues coming in from the little radio were so small. A cough, a rustle of paper, where there should have been complete silence. A spatter of applause that was surely too meagre for the size of the Assembly.

I bit my lip, and prayed. He spoke for just over an hour. It didn't seem that long. As he came to the climax I crouched close to the set.

"... So I plead with this World Assembly on behalf of those men and their families who during the last twenty-five years have gained a foothold on that most inhospitable planet, Moon. On behalf of those men who have won for Earth mineral riches beyond price I ask—Give us the freedom to determine our own future. Give us a seat on this Assembly. Give us a voice in the market-place, so that a fair price may be put on the minerals we mine for you, and so that the crippling charge of freight costs be removed from our backs, that we may enjoy a standard of living commensurate with Earth's. Accept us as a partner, rather than as a resource to be sucked dry and discarded. We Sellenites love Moon, and it is our home. But we never forget that Earth is our mother. Let us live together as a family and not become alienated for ever. Thank you."

The applause swelled and died. Through it I could hear the president calling on each nation to vote....

"Afghanistan." A rumbling voice in comment, into which the translation system crisply broke. I scrabbled in the inside pocket of my wetsuit. Yes, I had a waterproof tablet and stylo. I sat close to the radio ready to tally the vote ... "Yes."

"Albania ..." "No."

"Algeria ..." "Yes."

I tried to analyse the results as I listened and scored. It seemed as if the underdeveloped and agricultural nations were sympathetic with Moon's plea for self-determination, while the industrial nations, though they might sympathize, were voting "no", to protect their interests in our resources.

My mind ran over my text-tape on Earth Economy, and my heart sank. The industrial nations outnumbered the agricultural ones more than two to one. If the trend kept up we wouldn't stand a chance. Moon's struggle would go on, and I wasn't afraid of our ultimate victory. But the Conshelfers and the gillers would be lost before they had even begun.

Czechoslovakia and Denmark voted "yes" where I had expected "no", but otherwise there were no surprises. I looked at my watch. It was half past ten. With each delegate restricted to one minute's speech before his vote I had only till one o'clock, at the latest. It wasn't much time.

My plan had come to me complete in every detail in the moment when I had said goodbye to Hilary. It was two plans really, and I prayed that the first one would work, as I didn't feel very heroic. In fact the idea of putting my life on the line scared me spitless.

I took off my direction-finder sonar-alarm, and pried open

the back. As I had suspected it was similar to the devices we used on Moon. What I needed was some way of souping up the signal. There was only one place where I was going to find amplifiers, and that was inside the radio.

Iceland had just recorded its vote. The tally was still running two to one against Moon. I hated to cut off my only information channel, but later would be too late. I unscrewed the back, and found the transistors I was looking for.

Of course there was no way I could get my alarm-system back into its waterproof case. I struggled out of my wetsuit and took off my undershirt. I tore it into strips and carefully wrapped up the alarm, and put it in the waterproof bag that Hilary had left. One hour to go....

It was very quiet and lonely in my prison. I missed the voices on the radio as if they were personal friends. I glanced through my bubble walls. The occasional shadow of a fish drifted by, but I could see no sign of human life. I didn't really expect it. There were no need for guards. The water and the pressure made my prison secure.

I concentrated my mind on writing as concisely as possible the whole story of the giller rebellion, and their plan to sabotage the oil-rigs. I emphasized that the Conshelfers had nothing to do with it, and I explained how desperate the gillmen were for a fair hearing.

I addressed the letter to the World Intelligence Corps at the United Nations, and I sealed it with my father's seal, which he had given me when I was thirteen. This was the first time I had ever used it, and I looked solemnly at the image burned into the paper by the chemical action of the ring, the logos of the crescent moon and clasped hands. I prayed that the seal would do its work of getting the message to the right people fast.

I slipped the paper into the bag, touched off the souped-up alarm, and sealed the bag. The air would expand as the bag reached the less dense waters above, and by the time it hit the surface it would be like a visible balloon, emitting a signal audible to ships and planes alike.

I still had to get the device on its way. I realized with a shiver that I would have to swim away from the bubble in order to release it, or it might simply be trapped against the curved undersurface of the bubble. I scrambled back into my wetsuit, and sat down by the exit hole. I felt very naked without breathing gear. An additional danger struck me. How was I going to keep submerged at this depth? My natural buoyancy would pull me towards the surface. I had neither tanks nor belt to weigh me down.

I gritted my teeth and decided it was a risk I would have to take. I tucked the radio into the front of my wetsuit for ballast, and began to tear up the rest of my shirt into thin strips and knot them into some sort of rope. It was only about eight feet long, and horribly tatty and fragile, but it was the best I could do. I tied one end to the top rung of the ladder in the exit port, and the other to my left wrist.

Then I sat on the edge and breathed deeply, until my head began to spin. Now! I slid into the water and pushed with my arms to swim out and down. As far as I could go ... Let go the bag.

It shot out of my grasp and was gone in a second on its hundred foot ascent. Already I was bobbing like a cork against the side of the bubble six feet above the port. I tried to swim down, gently pulling myself in, praying the fragile line wouldn't break. Now I was back on the underside of the bubble. Now my hands could touch the ladder. And now, lungs bursting, I popped out of the water back into my prison. The line parted as I scrambled out of the water, but I had done it!

Half past twelve. Another half hour before the vote was in, and the fate of Moon and Ocean alike decided. I had a half hour to prepare my second plan, just in case.

I made another copy of the message I had sent to World

Intelligence. They would find it on my body, for this second plan was like that of the saboteur who walks into enemy headquarters with a grenade strapped to his own body. I prayed I wouldn't have to go through with it.

I had just hidden the paper inside my wetsuit, and was settling down to wait out the next fifteen minutes, when I was startled by the appearance of one of the gillmen.

He sprang half out of the water, like a dolphin, silvery wet and lithe, and he remained in the exit port, half in, half-out of the water, holding on to the ladder. I recognized the long darkly red hair, the slanting blue eyes, the straight nose and full mouth. It was my rescuer from the kelp bed, the leader of the gillmen, Hilary's brother Ian.

My heart was pounding as I got up and walked towards him. He flung up one silvery wet arm.

"That's enough. No nearer."

He spoke in a flat whisper, startlingly unresonant for such a big, deep-chested man. He ducked under, and as the hair floated back from his neck I could see the silvery-pink gill-membrane. He opened his mouth. The gills filled out, flushed pink. He surfaced, shaking the water from his eyes.

Then I realized that his chest wall never moved, that he didn't, in the accepted sense, breathe at all. I marvelled at the surgical skill that had made this adaptation possible. I was partly repulsed and partly attracted by him. But handsome or revolting, what a sacrifice to have made!

As I stared he moved abruptly and threw a package across the floor. It skidded on the smooth plastic and came to rest at my feet. I looked down and my heart sank. It was the bag with the alarm signal that I had sent to the surface no more than fifteen minutes ago. Plan One had failed, and now there was nothing left but Plan Two.

I stared defiantly at my jailor. He smiled back.

"Good marks for ingenuity," he whispered. "But you lost points through underestimating our technology. Just because we've returned to the water doesn't mean we have the brains of fish. We heard your signal the instant you released it, and sent a porpoise up to bring it back the minute it hit the surface."

He ducked under to breathe, and when he came up we began our strange dialogue. I had the feeling that I was indeed talking to a creature from another world. I had to remind myself constantly that he was indeed a man, that his adaptation was surgical, not mutant, and that it was to our common humanity that I must appeal, not to some alien ethic. I gave him all the arguments I'd given Hilary and then some more.

"You're almost as persuasive as your father. Where has it got him?"

"The vote?" My voice trembled.

"A tie when I left and the voting was nearly over."

My heart sank. Nothing but an overwhelming victory would persuade the gillmen to take the peaceful route. He must have read my face. He smiled, a surprisingly attractive smile that reminded me startlingly of Hilary.

"You're a good person, Kepler. I'm not surprised my sister likes you. But you're very naive. You just don't understand the depths of disinterest in what we of the ocean are trying to do for mankind. You can only jolt people out of apathy by shock tactics. And that's what we're going to have to use." He ducked below the water to breathe, and then went on.

"Listen. When the Conshelf projects started the world was spending 120 *billion* dollars a *year* on armaments—the research and manufacture of more efficient ways of killing off mankind. At that time one thousandth of that amount was being spent on all aspects of oceanic research. In the last thirty years the expenditure on armaments has gone up ten times, and so has the amount spent on oceanic research. It still seems to the Topside governments a thousand times more important to develop bigger and better weapons than it does to learn the secrets of the ocean that covers almost three-quarters of our globe. We have to learn how to farm fish and seaweeds, how to adapt the ocean currents to clean our rivers and shores, how to increase the oxygen emission of the ocean to replace that lost for ever in the combustion processes of industry.

"There is so much to do, and it's going to take men that are determined and dedicated, unafraid to give their whole lives to the search for knowledge in the ocean depths. We've made the big jump into the new environment while the scientists Topside are still talking and talking and wasting Earth's resources. We've proved that life under the sea is possible, and nobody will listen. Nobody cares."

I was exhausted and discouraged, and unthinkingly I said the first thing that came into my head.

"You must be so lonely."

His head jerked and his mouth twisted. His eyes, so like Hilary's in colour and shape, were dull and filmy, where hers would sparkle as if, even under sixty feet of water, they caught the sun.

"I ... I'm sorry," I stammered. "But I wonder if the real reason you're turning to violence is because apathy is so alienating? You have to be noticed, you have to make them aware of you, because you are so alone?"

"We are so small in the great ocean," he whispered. "We are like tiny shrimps borne along in a sea of plankton. The ocean is vast and we are so unimportant. When I see the shadows of the big fish I cringe and hide against a rock like a damsel fish in the coral. It was never like that when I was a skin-diver."

"Was it so when you were first changed?"

"Oh, no. It was beautiful. It was freedom from tanks and masks and pressure gauges. Oh, we still can't sound from the depths to the surface like a porpoise or a whale. But since our lungs are no longer filled with gases we are free of a couple of hundred feet of vertical flying space. Can you imagine it?"

"I used to dream of flying when I was a boy. Did you? Perhaps we all do. You know what I think? ... I think it's a race memory, but nothing to do with bird flight. I think it's a memory of the ocean life we once enjoyed, the three-dimensional freedom that the first amphibians sacrificed when they crept on to the harsh surface of the land and committed themselves to the force of gravity for ever."

"Aren't you exaggerating?" I wondered if he were quite sane.

"Am I? Do you know how close you still are to your mother the Ocean? Your bloodstream is a sea with the elements of sodium, potassium and calcium combined in a watery fluid identical to that of the ocean of 300 million years ago. For nine months before your birth you lived in a miniature ocean. At one period in your embryonic life you even had gills, Kepler. Gills like these." He touched his neck.

"If we are so close to the ocean as you say, then what went wrong with your adaptation?"

"I ... I don't know. It came slowly. A feeling of loneliness, of insecurity. Separation." He looked across at me and I was startled to see tears in his eyes. I glanced away, but he saw my expression and smiled wryly.

"Yes, I can still weep, Kepler. There's an old Earth tradition that mermen and mermaids couldn't weep, because they had no souls. I am still human. I still have a soul."

"I know you're human, Ian. I want to help you, so much. But I know that what you're planning is all wrong."

" 'Under the sea everything is moral,' " Ian quoted. "We are very sensitive to what is right and wrong, Kepler, perhaps more than Topsiders. There'll be no loss of life in our rebellion, I promise you."

"But I think to Topsiders property is as important as life—maybe more so. There are certainly more laws to protect it. If you destroy those oil-wells your act will be considered as violent as if you'd killed."

133

Ian moved his hands in a gesture of hopelessness. "What can I do. I have no other weapon. I have no act or idea strong enough to make the Topsiders realize how desperately important our freedom is to us. No, it's too late. Our plans are made. To give up now would be to destroy us utterly."

He turned away from the ladder and I was afraid he was leaving. I knelt by the exit port and when he surfaced again I grasped his wrist. The flesh was warm, and this startled me. Had I really expected him to be cold like a fish? No wonder he felt alien, if this was how I reacted to him.

"Don't go, Ian. I have an idea that may help you."

He looked up with such hope in his eyes that I knew then that the hate he had felt towards the Topsiders after the death of his father was no longer a living thing, but a dying fire that he fanned into reluctant flame to keep him warm in the dark and lonely deeps.

I spoke rapidly, the whole plan clear in my head, as if I were reading it off a text-tape.

"I must talk to all of you, somewhere outside of this place. If you could get me an air-tank, and some sort of intercom. Whatever you use for communicating. It'll work, Ian. I know it'll work. I have your idea and your act to make Topside realize just how serious you are."

My excitement was catching. Ian nodded.

"I'll be back." He was gone in a swirl of bubbles, and I sat down to add a vital footnote to my message to World Intelligence.

Then I got the alarm signal out of its watertight bag. It took only a minute to detach the amplifiers and restore the original device to its case and put it back on my wrist. I twisted it around so that I could touch off the porpoise signal with my middle finger without the movement being noticed.

Ian returned with a breather pack over one shoulder. He gave me a face-mask and a device to strap on my throat so that I could talk to the gillers. But I noticed that he gave me no flippers, nor did he strap the breather pack on my back.

"I'm taking no chances with you, my slippery young friend. Come on."

He handed me the mouthpiece, and with his arm around my shoulders we slipped into the water together. We swam along for about fifty yards, passing the shadowy forms of strangely shaped dwellings, to a natural arena formed from a rocky basin. It was crowded with gillmen, more than I would have believed possible.

I was horribly afraid. Everything hung on how far away the nearest porpoise was, and how soon after getting to me it would have to surface. My natural buoyancy kept trying to lift me away from Ian and the breather pack, and I had to keep a tight grip on Ian's arm.

I took a deep breath and began to talk to the gillers. I repeated what I had said to Ian. Then my left hand closed and my finger felt out the porpoise caller. There. Nobody saw anything. I went on talking.

"You need an act that is strong enough to wake Topside out of its apathy. To make the ordinary people aware of the special needs of both Conshelfers and gillmen. I agree with you. But that act doesn't have to be an act of violence. I have a better idea."

Out of the corner of my face-mask I could see an approaching shadow. I dared not turn my head, but went on talking.

"I am from Moon. I have no personal stake in your future in the ocean. If I involve myself it is because I believe in the justice of your claims, and *that* Earth is bound to notice."

The porpoise butted impatiently at my side. Slowly I put out my left hand to caress it.

"So I offer myself as that act which will make the Topsiders aware of your needs."

Nobody moved. I took a last deep breath, spat out the mouthpiece and let go Ian's arm. The porpoise stirred. I grasped its dorsal fin with both hands and we were off, soaring upwards towards the light, fast, faster than any gillman could possibly follow.

CHAPTER TWELVE

Even in that moment of utmost danger the thing I felt most was the incredible joy of that soaring flight on the porpoise's back. I lay along its body, holding the dorsal fin with both hands, my legs around its tail, and I could feel the surge of its muscles through my whole body. I had thought skin-diving was a wonderful experience, but it was like crawling on all fours compared to this rapturous ride. I had a sense of union with the water, a feeling of power and rightness.

I remembered Hilary's warnings of what could happen to a man's lungs as the gases within them expanded in response to the lessening atmospheric pressure outside, until they could pop like a soggy balloon. I exhaled slowly and carefully as we soared upwards.

The dark greys gave place to blues, blue-greens to a momentary dazzling gold, and then we were through, breathing clean fresh air just when I felt I couldn't hold out for another second. The sun was noon-high and golden, and it smote at my unaccustomed face like a blow. I shut my eyes and lay back on the surface of the sea, my arm across the porpoise's back. The water moved lazily under my body, breathing like a living creature. Languidly I lifted my arm and turned my sonar alarm to maximum gain.

The world was a hemisphere of golden dazzling silence. My porpoise slid under the water, dived, rolled and came back to me. The golden drops splashed from its body back into the sea without a sound. A shadow winged overhead. I looked up to see the silver arrow of a supersonic jet arching across the sky. I felt the pressure-wave against my skin, but I heard nothing. I shouted, clapped my hands together ... all was silence. Puzzled, I put my hands to my ears and brought them away smeared with blood.

I was beginning to feel very tired. How soon would my alarm be detected? The skin on my arms and legs was itching unbearably. I remembered seeing a man rescued from a blow-out on Moon. He had screamed that he was being eaten alive by red ants. I knew now just how he felt.

I whistled the porpoise to me, and it came, obedient but puzzled. Though it was trained to help humans I was not behaving in the normal pattern of Conshelfers or gillmen. Would it stay on the surface and hold me up till help came? I hooked my arm over its back and stroked its firm wet skin. I tried to talk to it, but the strange noises that started in my head were too disturbing and I gave up the attempt.

Quite without warning the pain struck. I must have screamed out loud, for the body of the porpoise flinched against me. The pain hit my left knee and ankle first. Then my right leg. And my left elbow, the one I'd banged on a rock a few days before. I couldn't hold on any longer. I slid under the water and choked on a salty mouthful.

I managed to struggle up again. Was that the bow-wave of a boat over there? Or just spin-drift blowing off a wave top? I had to hang on ... just long enough for them to reach my body and find the message. I fought the pain and weakness. Then a stab like a knife came in my side and I choked and went under.

What happened afterwards must have been a dream. Or was I partly awake? A song kept going through my head, and I was moving smoothly along to its rhythm. It was from *The Tempest*, which I'd studied in Moon school, an odd choice of play for a planet with neither wind nor water.

"Full fathom five thy father lies,
Of his bones are coral made.
Those are pearls that were his eyes.
Nothing of him does remain
But has suffered a sea-change
Into something rich and strange."

The gillers had suffered a sea-change, and now I had joined them. I seemed to see my arms and legs transmuted into beautiful pink-red coral, and that I was being drawn in a crystal casket through the water by a crowd of mermen. I could see the silver of their tails, and the gills moving softly like seaweed. I lay in wonder in a silent pain-free world, tranquil and unafraid. Then I must have drifted into sleep, for the dream ended.

Later I remembered being held and lifted by many hands, firm and gentle. There was a wonderful feeling of trust. I lay still and let whatever happen, happen.

When I woke up next I knew with certainty that a long, long time had gone by. I was lying on my back in bed, a bed whose mattress had been tilted to the exact angle for comfort. A hospital? I looked around. The room was small, squarish, and there were no windows. Above my bed was a ventilator grille, the tell-tale fronds of plastic lifting and rippling in the stream of in-coming air. I wasn't Topside then. Was I on the Conshelf, or back on Moon?

I heard the footsteps in the passage outside, and suddenly realized that I was *hearing* them. I was alive. I could move my arms and legs, and I could hear again!

When the doctor came into the room I was grinning from ear to ear. It was Dr. McIntosh. I was back home on Conshelf Ten.

"How did I ... ? What happened ... ?"

"Take it easy now. All in good time. You've had a grand sleep, but you'd better not bounce around like that. Aye, the gillers brought you in. They went right up to the surface after you and brought you straight back here. It saved your life. Getting you straight back to depth was quicker and safer than any decompression chamber Topside, and here we have better facilities.

"No, I don't think you'll have any permanent damage in your joints ... maybe a spot of arthritis in old age. The worst damage was an embolism in your lung. If they'd got to you a minute later, that would have been that. Man, that was a reckless thing you did! ... Yes, both your ear-drums were perforated, but they've healed up nicely in the week you've been here.... Aye, it's been a whole week. I've never seen a man sleep so well. We've been feeding you intravenously, but I'll bet you're about ready for a square meal. I'll just send your special nurse in with it."

After he left I lay back, my head in a whirl. A special nurse? I was certainly getting the red-carpet treatment ... I thought of Father, and it all came back to me. The vote? The giller rebellion? My note to the U.N.? A whole week. I'd been asleep a whole *week*! Why, nowadays, the whole course of history could change in a week.

I waited in a fever of impatience for someone to come on whom I could unload my questions. It seemed like hours before the door was pushed open and my nurse entered. She pulled across the bedside table, put down the tray and then gave me a most unprofessional kiss. It was Hilary! Special nurse indeed!

"You look really good, Kepler."

"So do you, Hilary." Even with her spectacular hair rolled up and hidden under a white cap she was still the most beautiful person I had ever seen. "Hilary, for goodness' sake tell me what's been happening. I don't even know what questions to ask!"

"I know. Don't worry. Just eat and I'll talk. First off, though, everything is absolutely okay."

So I sat up in bed and ate my first meal in a week while Hilary brought me up to date.

"Well, first of all Ian and the other gillers brought you right in to Conshelf Ten. I phoned ahead from one of the way-stations to explain what had happened, so the Conshelfers didn't think that the gillers were invading them! As soon as they got you out of your wetsuit they found the letter, and the Controller 'faxed' it in to the U.N. Then he went out to talk to the gillers. I was still out there with Ian and the others then. We thought you'd gone mad, you know, pulling a stunt like that. But when the Controller read your letter we realized what you'd done for us all. There was no question any more of sabotaging the oil-rigs. We told the Controller that and he went in and phoned the U.N. They told him then that when your message was read out in the General Assembly the delegates stood up and cheered."

I remembered what I had written in that hasty postscript, and I flushed to the roots of my hair. I had said. "I offer my life as an act to bring to the attention of this World Body the inequities suffered by those who have dedicated their lives to colonizing the seas for the benefit of all mankind."

At that moment when I thought I was going to my death it had seemed the fitting thing to say. Now, a week later, I blushed for my heroics.

"Anyway," Hilary went on, "when the delegates stopped cheering, someone proposed a special session to investigate the status of Conshelfers and gillers. It was passed unanimously. Ian sent word to his people to disarm the oil-rigs and return all the explosives to Conshelf Ten. He's been talking to Dr. McIntosh, and they've worked out a plan to send down a team of psychologists to discover the reasons for the emotional changes the gillers have experienced, and see what can be done about them."

"What about Father?"

"He's fine. Of course he's been worried for you. But once

he knew you were out of danger he was very happy. Of course gaining Moon autonomy was a great thing!"

"But the vote was going against us ... ?

"Moon won by a narrow margin. It was so narrow that your father stood up in the Assembly and said that it was such a grudging mandate that he couldn't possibly accept it. He was ready to pack up and leave for Moon immediately. The President called for a second vote, and this time it was overwhelmingly in favour of Moon's independence. He's quite a guy, your father."

"I know."

"So's his son. Kep, I wonder how we can ever thank you enough for all you've done for us."

"Forget it, please. I can't begin to tell you what life on the Conshelf has done for *me*. Hilary, what about you? Your part in the rebellion?"

"It's all right. Conshelfers aren't vindictive. I'm forgiven. The worst punishment was thinking that even indirectly I was responsible for your death, or crippling. But that's over now.... Your father plans to go back to Moon earlier than he originally planned, now that things have worked out so well. He plans to go in about a month. Will you go with him?"

"Will I?" I looked across at Hilary curled up in a very unnurselike position on the bottom of the bed. "I wish you'd take off that silly cap."

She laughed and pulled it off, and her hair tumbled down in a cascade over her shoulders. I picked up a tress of it and let it slide through my fingers. I sighed.

"I never did dance with you at the bottom of the sea."

"No, you never did."

"And I've never explored the coral beds of the Caribbean."

"No, Kepler."

I thought of my struggle to stay alive on the ocean surface. That wasn't for myself, but for the Conshelfers and the gillers.

I thought of my father pleading before the General Assembly for self-determination for Moon, and I knew that he too hadn't done it for himself. It was for me. For my children.

"Would you come with me to Moon, Hilary?"

She shook her head. "I'd be a fish out of water, literally, Kep. My home is down here."

"I have to go."

"Yes, I know Your girl ... Ann ... she'll be waiting for you?"

"Yes. And you? Is it going to be all right between you and Jon?"

"I think so. I hope so. He's a forgiving sort of guy."

"I'll think of you often. Be happy, Hilary."

"You too, Kep."

She brushed my lips with hers and ran out of the room. We met many times during the next three weeks, but that was our last private moment together. Finally came a day of goodbyes, and Dr. McIntosh and I went by sled to the decompression chamber off the coast.

Forty-eight hours later, and Father and I were face to face again. It had only been a few months, and yet as we hugged each other I knew, and I knew that he knew, that I had gone down into the sea a brash kid, and that now I had come back a man.

We took the plush Earth-ferry up to Space Station. There was the usual delay before the Moon-ferry left, and I went straight out to the Earth viewport.

The shapes of Africa and India moved under my eyes. I never had got to see the Sphinx or the Taj Mahal, but I had no regrets. I had found something much more important.... The blue expanse of Earth's oceans, whirled over with whip-cream cloud patterns, passed below....

When Icarus put on wings he thought he was as great as the gods and he tried to fly to the sun. For his pride his wings were melted off and he fell into the sea and was drowned.

My people had put on wings and gone to the Moon. One day perhaps we would reach out to the planets. Maybe my son. Or his son.

Ian and his people had exchanged lungs for gills and ventured into the ocean where no unprotected man had dared before. How would they make out? Would they continue to remember their humanity? Would we?

I thought lovingly of Hilary, her courage and her beauty. Then I turned my back on Earth and went across the Space Station concourse to the far side, where I could look towards home.

Moon was full. In the silver radiance I couldn't see the shadow of Kepler's crater. But I knew where it was, there, where the rays of Copernicus fanned out, like the feelers of an anemone, like a starfish. Ann was down there. I could think of her and Hilary together without any sense of disloyalty.

It was as if I had gone on a wonderful glamorous voyage. It was something I would remember the rest of my life, and the memory would bring warmth and colour to any dark times that might lie ahead. And I knew that it was when I was back home, with Ann, that these memories would mean the most. It was to Home that I was going now.